A Tale of the Secret Saint ZERO

NOVEL 2

WRITTEN BY
Touya

ILLUSTRATED BY
chibi

Airship

Seven Seas Entertainment

Tensei Sita Daiseijyo ha, Seijyo dearuko towohitakakusu ZERO Volume 2

Originally published in Japan in 2023
by EARTH STAR Entertainment, Tokyo.
English translation rights arranged
with EARTH STAR Entertainment, Tokyo,
through TOHAN CORPORATION, Tokyo.

Seven Seas press and purchase enquiries can be sent to Marketing Manager Lauren Hill at press@gomanga.com. Information regarding the distribution and purchase of digital editions is available from Digital Operations Manager CK Russell at digital@gomanga.com.

Follow Seven Seas Entertainment online at sevenseasentertainment.com.

TRANSLATION: Kim Morrissy
ADAPTATION: Melanie Kardas
LOGO & COVER DESIGN: Nicky Lim
INTERIOR LAYOUT & DESIGN: Clay Gardner
COPY EDITOR: Jade Gardner
PROOFREADER: Meg van Huygen
EDITOR: Laurel Ashgrove
PREPRESS TECHNICIAN: Salvador Chan Jr., April Malig, Jules Valera
MANAGING EDITOR: Alyssa Scavetta
EDITOR-IN-CHIEF: Julie Davis
PUBLISHER: Lianne Sentar
VICE PRESIDENT: Adam Arnold
PRESIDENT: Jason DeAngelis

ISBN: 979-8-89160-945-7
Printed in Canada
First Printing: May 2025
10 9 8 7 6 5 4 3 2 1

THE STORY THUS FAR

SERAFINA, THE YOUNGEST PRINCESS of the Náv Kingdom, was born blind. For six years, she was hidden away in a forest, where she lived peacefully with young spirits as her friends. Then one day, out of the blue, a visitor arrived from the capital.

"You must be Serafina. I am your cousin, Sirius Ulysses."

The young knight brigade vice-commander chose to remain with Serafina in the forest for a while instead of forcing her back to the royal capital. But in a twist of fate, she gained her sight—unleashing an extraordinary power at the same time.

With that, Serafina moved to the capital with Sirius, reunited with her family, and began a new life.

Character List

SERAFINA NÁV

The second princess of Náv. Has crimson hair and golden eyes. She lived hidden away in the Forest of Lent because of her blindness since birth, but she returned to the royal capital after regaining her sight. Despite her tender age, she already possesses exceptional ability as a saint.

SIRIUS ULYSSES

Vice-commander of the Náv Horned Beast Knights at the young age of nineteen. Current head of the Ulysses dukedom and nephew to the king. A handsome man with gray hair and silver eyes, he is the kingdom's strongest swordsman.

SEVEN

A young spirit boy who has a pact with Serafina.

CANOPUS BLAZEJ

A young man from the islander minority group. After Serafina chose him as her personal knight, he swore an oath of fealty to her.

SCHEAT KNOWLES

Formerly belonged to the First Knight Brigade, but was transferred to the Royal Red Shield. A cheerful and boisterous knight with red and golden hair.

MIRACH QUARK

Formerly belonged to the Second Knight Brigade, but was transferred to the Royal Red Shield. A caring and helpful knight with a slender physique and baby face.

Procyon Náv
Serafina's father. The king.

Spica Náv
Serafina's mother. The queen.

Vega Náv
Serafina's older brother. The first prince.

Capella Náv
Serafina's older brother. The second prince.

Rigel Náv
Serafina's older brother. The third prince.

Shaula Náv
Serafina's older sister. The first princess.

Wezen Wald
Captain of the Náv Horned Beast Knights. A gallant and highly respected man, yet terrible at paperwork.

Deneb Bonino
Former captain of the Second Knight Brigade. Was reassigned to captain of the Royal Red Shield.

Miaplacidus Ames
Formerly belonged to the First Knight Brigade, but was transferred to the Royal Red Shield. A brawny and masculine knight.

Náv Kingdom Royal Family Tree

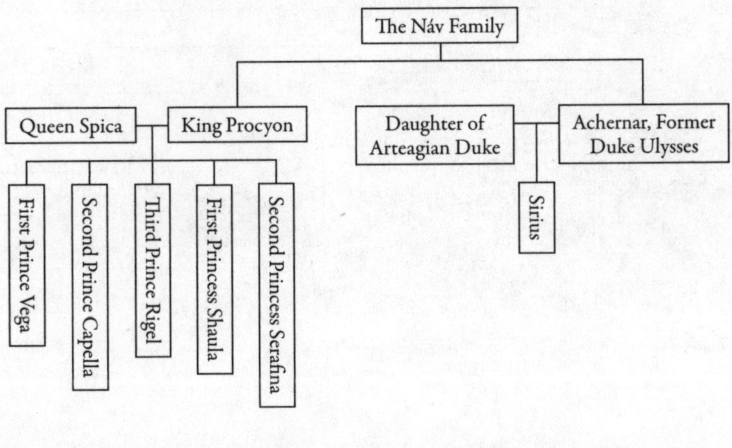

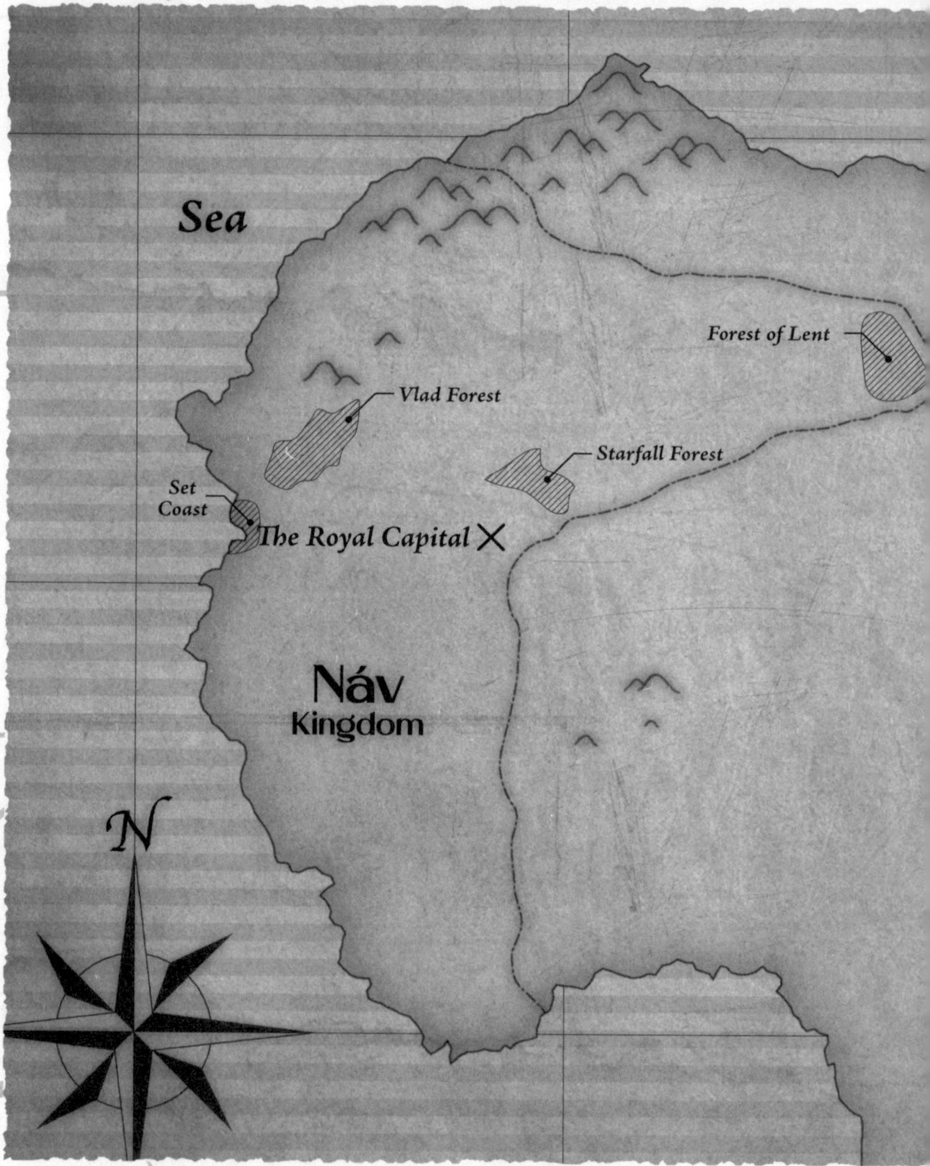
Sea
Forest of Lent
Vlad Forest
Starfall Forest
Set
Coast
The Royal Capital
Náv
Kingdom
N

The Arteaga Empire
Entire Continent
Kingdom
Empire

NÁV KNIGHT BRIGADE

Commander	Wezen Wald
Vice-Commander	Sirius Ulysses
First Knight Brigade Captain	Kaus Australis

ROYAL RED SHIELD

Captain	Deneb Bonino
Serafina's Personal Knight	Scheat Knowles Mirach Quark Miaplacidus Ames
Personal Knight	Canopus Blazej

The Little Saint and a Knight's Vow

"OKAY, THEN I'LL BE your saint!"

The morning after I said that to Sirius, I woke up before Seven stirred me for once. I was bubbling with excitement about taking a bold new step as a saint.

It's been my dream to be a saint ever since I was little. Nothing has ever swayed me from that path, but meeting Sirius made me want to use my powers to protect *him*. When I begged him to let me fight alongside him last night, he answered with a coolheaded suggestion: Ask the king for permission to train as a saint.

So we were heading to see Father today. Exciting, right? I bet that's why I woke up earlier than usual.

Sirius came to pick me up after I got dressed and had breakfast. I did one last look over my outfit, and then we were off. As we walked down the long corridor, he peered down at me.

"Just checking," he said, "but last night, you said you were determined to become a saint, age be damned. Now, I know that you tend to get fired up in the evenings, so I want to know: Do you still feel the same way after a night's sleep?"

Gosh, was there even any point in asking that?

"You bet!" I chirped. "I've wanted to be a saint since forever. A bit of sleep won't change that! Besides, I don't think while I'm asleep. Why would my feelings change?"

Sirius flinched as if what I said hadn't even occurred to him. "Right... A night is a long time for me but not necessarily for you. You always fall asleep as soon as your head hits the pillow, and you never open your eyes until your spirit shakes you awake. The time between night and morning might as well be nothing."

Yup, he got it. "Just checking," I said, copying him. "If Father gives his permission and I become an awesome saint, will you let me fight with you?"

Sirius nodded with a straight face. "Yes, I promised you that last night," he said crisply. "I never break promises."

Awesome! I took his hand and swung it uuuuup and down. This caused the knights guarding the hallway to stare at us in shock, so I stopped doing it. *Oh no,* I told myself. *I have to be ultra-modest if I'm gonna (maybe) be an awesome saint on the battlefield.*

I tried to walk gracefully with a proper dignified expression, but that didn't last long, since Sirius picked me up and carried me down the hall. He must have thought I was nervous because I wasn't acting like my usual self.

Jeez, I thought, feeling a headache creep up on me. *Maybe Sirius is the biggest block to my "act like a dignified saint" plan.*

◇◇◇

Father was in the middle of receiving a report from some other nobles when the two of us—the overprotective knight and the dignified princess—entered his study. A servant told me to sit on the sofa while I waited; it seemed like it was going to take a while.

When Father spotted me swinging my legs to pass the time, his bored expression completely changed. "Okay!" he said, turning to the three nobles reporting to him. "What a great idea you have! Why, it was so novel that I didn't understand it one bit, but hey, you should give it a try. Talk to me again when you have the results."

The nobles' eyes boggled.

"Huh? But we haven't finished explaining our plan! I mean, we only just got started. Are you sure that was enough for you to make a decision?"

"And you're telling us to go ahead? When there hasn't been a single precedent?!"

They looked bewildered that the king approved their idea without even looking at their paperwork. But Father just nodded lightly. "Yup, go knock yourselves out! Off you go."

Oh dear, was this really how you were supposed to run a kingdom? I looked up at Sirius worriedly, but he just shrugged.

"Pretty much any idea has only about a ten percent chance of succeeding. Deciding on public policy is like gambling in some ways...but I will say that King Procyon's judgment is remarkably keen compared to past monarchs throughout history. He may appear frivolous, but his mind is quick, and he has a firm grasp on what information he needs to make his decisions. His intuition can be scarily accurate."

"Wow, that's my daddy for you!" I clapped my hands together in delight.

Sirius nodded in agreement. "Yes. His eyes might not be as vibrant as yours, but I expect that he received some manner of blessing from the Spirit Lord too. Well, that, or he might just have good intuition."

The nobles left the room as we were talking. When they were gone, Father approached us with a broad grin on his face.

"You never change, Sirius," he said. "I admire your pluck, saying exactly what you think about people while they're within earshot. And about your king, no less! But you had nice things to say, so I'll let you off the hook." He sat down on the sofa across from us. "So what did you two come here for so early in the morning? Don't expect me to say yes if you're asking my permission to marry her."

I grinned at Father's stern face. "Glad you shot that down, since I want something else! Can I be a saint? You'll say yes to that, right?"

"What? But you're only six! It's too soon for you to start training..." Father was about to object, but he cut himself off as if a thought had just occurred to him. "Oh, I get it. You might not yet be an adult, but you already have a spirit pact. It's *technically* possible for you to work as a saint right now. But still, you're six! That's way too young to have such a position."

Father looked unsure, so I stood up from the sofa and started begging. "But, Father, there might be other people like me who were born blind! I wanna help them right now, not in nine years when I become a grown-up. I bet they can't fully enjoy life in complete darkness."

Especially if they didn't have spirit friends like I did.

Father's eyes welled up with tears as he listened to me. "Oh, Serafina! You're so compassionate!" he declared, nodding fervently. "Oh, how greatly you must have suffered when you couldn't see! I can tell how much this means to you. What kind of father would I be if I didn't grant your greatest wish? Honestly, you're such a sweet girl, it's lighting a fire in me. All right, I'll allow you to become a saint! But you mustn't overdo it, you hear? You wouldn't want it to get in the way of your education as a princess."

Seeing my daddy look so weepy caused me to run up to him all wishy-washy. To be completely honest, I didn't really care about becoming a good princess. I would rather train hard and become a strong saint instead of studying, but I knew that my parents wanted me to grow up as proper royalty after all that time I spent at the villa—so I nodded in agreement to his wishes.

Then I gave Father a biiiig hug. "Thank you, Father! I'm gonna work hard to become an awesome saint! Once I do, I'll fight alongside Sirius!"

"What?! H-hold on a second, Serafina! What was that last part you said?! Don't tell me you want to be a saint on the battlefield, not one that helps behind the scenes?! And you want to be on the *front lines* with Sirius?!" He looked at me, astonished.

"Yep!" I answered with a smile. "I know I can't do it right away, but when I'm all trained up, Sirius is gonna take me to battle!"

But then, for some reason, Father stared back at me with a pale face.

"No! No, no, no, no, no, *no*!" he said over and over, like he was chanting something. He threw a glare at Sirius. "S-Sirius! The knight brigade already has plenty of saints! Can't *they* take care of you?! What do you need little Serafina for?! Argh, don't tell me you get off on being protected by small children!"

Sirius scowled. "Your Majesty, could you quit it with the tasteless jokes? I'd want Serafina to protect me because her skills exceed the other saints. It's why I personally would like to see her walk that path. If she trains and adjusts well to the battlefield, then I'd like her to fight with me. Bu it goes without saying that I would protect her with my life. Like you, I was worried about her age...but I believe that her skills are peerless. So there's no reason to stop her."

As he spoke, Sirius gazed straight into Father's eyes and then bowed his head solemnly.

"Please allow us to fight together."

Hurriedly, I bowed my head too and clapped my hands together. "Please, Father!"

Silence fell over the room for a while, then Father spoke in a tear-choked voice. "Ohhh, Serafina! You've already grown up so nicely! How beautiful! Daddy's getting emotional!" He sniffed loudly and hugged me tightly. "If you ever get fed up training with Sirius, just know that you can quit being a battlefield saint anytime! Saints who specialize in curing illnesses are just as respectable, and so are the ones who make healing potions!

Honestly, since you're a princess and all, you don't even *need* to work as a saint!"

"So you're saying I can fight with Sirius?" I asked, not certain if he was giving me his permission or not.

Father nodded, his face streaked with tears. "Of course you can. You're only six, but you've already made such a noble decision. How could I not respect that? And don't you worry! I might not look it, but your daddy was a knight around twenty years ago. If push comes to shove, I can fight alongside you too!"

Sirius looked *very* displeased with those words, but he wisely kept his silence.

Father continued in a hushed tone: "I'm giving the okay because it's the single thing you're asking for, Serafina. I would have thrown Sirius out the door if *he* asked me. I don't like how he always comes to me with *facts* and *logic*! When he does things the right way and comes to me with a sound argument, it makes me look like the bad guy for getting in his way. It's plain unfair that he can be a hero who contributes so much to the kingdom *and* has a proper head on his shoulders!"

After his spiel, he loosened his embrace and looked me in the eye.

"It's ideal that people take on responsibilities that match their talents, but you don't *have* to live life that way. Don't forget that you're only six. You don't need to put yourself through hell at your age. On top of all that, you're a princess—it's fine if you're pampered."

"Father..." It made me so happy to know that he was thinking about me. My heart swelled with emotion.

"Shaula has red hair just like you, but she isn't going out of her way to make her life difficult," Father went on earnestly. "To me, you are both my cute daughters. I'm going to raise you to be the best princesses you can, no matter what path you take!"

He turned and glared at Sirius again.

"Sirius, Serafina is Náv's second princess! You'd better treat her nicer than your beloved sword *and* your precious knights!"

"I'm quite aware of the situation. Serafina is more precious than anything in the world. I would never treat anyone or anything with more care." Sirius paused and then added, "Oh, Your Majesty, I'd like to ask one more thing of you."

"Huh? You're still not done? I never pegged you as such an avaricious man, Sirius!" Father complained with a scowl.

Sirius didn't look like he minded one bit as he launched straight into his request. "I would like to swear a knight's vow to Serafina."

The statement took Father by such surprise that his jaw dropped, and he stared blankly at Sirius. "What?" he said, after a very long pause.

But he seemed to quickly pull himself together, and he held up both his hands as if trying to keep Sirius in check.

"Hold on! Wait just a second here! What is the meaning of this? Yes, I know that swearing a knight's vow would be the highest honor to Serafina, but...just think about it! Doing that means you'd have to be joined at the hip with her at all times. And you're *fine* with that?" Father folded his arms and shook his head furiously. "You'd stand out too much. If you're backing Serafina, it would look to all the world that she's secretly in charge of the kingdom!"

"You're overthinking this. I simply want to be Serafina's knight."

"And that's the problem! If you swear fealty to her, then every single knight in the brigade will be obliged to do the same! Your popularity with the common people would influence their opinion too! Everyone would put Serafina on a pedestal!" Father countered frantically.

Sirius looked at him coldly, unamused by what he clearly thought was an exaggeration. "Your concerns are reasonable, but given that Serafina is a princess, she was always going to attract attention. I expect there would only be a slight stir if she were to become my lady."

"Oh, you fool! Don't you realize how popular you are! You're underestimating your influence by a country mile! Oh, and don't casually drop things like 'my lady' into conversation! I didn't know such swoon-worthy phrases were even in your vocabulary! Anyone hearing *you* say that with your handsome face is going to have their heart explode and die! Next time you pull that stunt, I'm going to punish you for the crime of being too damn sexy!"

As Father went on a hard-to-understand rant, Sirius stood up wordlessly and did a small bow. "I thank you for lending us your valuable time. I appreciate that you've entrusted Serafina to me, and I vow to protect her with all my might as her knight."

"Hold it right there, you!" Father spoke up, flustered. "Sure, I'm allowing Serafina to fight as a saint, but since when did I entrust her to *you*? Don't you dare treat this as a guaranteed thing! Darn it, Sirius, are you listening to me?!"

"She will be in safe hands," Sirius replied smoothly. "Regardless of whether I make the vow, I *will* be her knight, and I will protect her with my life. Now then, I'm sure you're a busy man, Your Majesty, so please allow me to excuse myself."

When he was done saying his piece, he plucked me out of Father's arms and left the king's study with a bow. Father shouted something loudly all the while, but Sirius didn't slow down a single bit. He strode down the hallway without even waiting for the study door to close.

I turned to face him, cocking my head. "Father gave his permission, right? That means I can go to battle with you if I work hard and become an awesome saint?"

Although I was right there when the topic came up, there were so many other topics thrown in that I couldn't really follow the conversation.

Sirius stopped and, in a very calm and dignified voice, answered, "Yes, you have his permission. By the way, Serafina, I have an ideal fighting method that I've dreamed of for many years. I don't intend to push it onto you, but in your very first battle, you showed me something that surpassed my wishful thinking. What I'm trying to say is that you're already more than capable. You don't have to push yourself further. I'm the one who should be striving to be better, so that I can protect you as a knight."

"Oh, yippee! A compliment from the national hero!" I clapped my hands in joy. I couldn't fully wrap my head around everything Sirius was saying, but I could tell it was something nice about me.

Sirius fell silent for a moment, then lifted me up even higher, moving me from his chest to sit on his shoulders. "A princess with such a good reputation deserves a special seat."

"Tee hee hee hee!" I giggled, enjoying the view from the top.

Sirius peered up at me in amusement. "I'll have to rethink the knights' configuration if you're going to fight as a saint. There's already a royal guard assembled, but I'll need more people with combat experience."

"Like Canopus?"

"Yes, like him," he agreed smoothly. "I'll show off your guards next time we meet. Look forward to it, Serafina. I'll be pulling out all the stops."

He looked like he was relishing the task in front of him as he dropped me off at my chamber. He walked off, smiling openly for once. It's hard to say, but maybe he was really happy when Father gave his permission.

I waved at Sirius's back before looking up at Canopus, who had been following us this whole time. "Did you hear? Sirius is gonna make the awesomest royal guard ever. I can't wait!"

"I must apologize for contradicting you, but I cannot say that I look forward to it whatsoever. I am filled with dread."

Unlike Sirius, who was over the moon, Canopus had a dead serious look on his face, and his large body was trembling.

I couldn't help but giggle at the huge difference between them. "Oh, Canopus! There can't be *that* many knights on your level. I bet Sirius was joking."

That's what I genuinely thought at the time...but I didn't know any better. Sirius sometimes made clumsy jokes, but he never joked when he made a *promise*. And because I didn't have a clue, I laughed at Canopus and said it was all a funny joke.

As it turned out, peace is built on ignorance.

Genesis of the Royal Red Shield

"YOUR HIGHNESS Princess Serafina Náv, may I ask you to accompany me?"

I was sitting on a chair in my room, opening my mouth wide to devour a cookie, when Sirius showed up talking like an entirely different person.

As curious as I was about what was going on with him, the plate full of cookies looked a lot more appetizing. I couldn't leave Sirius waiting, but I could tell that I wouldn't be able to have the rest if I didn't finish them off right now. I just knew a lady-in-waiting would pack the whole plate away.

This was the big issue on my mind as I stuffed a cookie into my mouth with one hand and crammed the rest into my dress pocket with the other.

Sirius watched this whole chain of actions without saying a word, although he did let out an unmistakable sigh. I didn't understand it, really. Here I was, showing off my slick skills by storing up my cookies *and* going along with his request at the same time. So why was he looking at me as if I'd done something naughty?

Sirius's look annoyed me, but I was too busy wondering whether I should lick the cookie crumbles off my fingers to say anything about it. I was still trying to make up my mind when Sirius pulled a handkerchief out of his pocket and wiped my hands. Then, with a very refined and dignified motion, he extended his white-gloved hand toward me.

"How do you fare, Your Highness?"

I wondered if this was a game Sirius was playing—maybe a "don't stop being polite" one? As confused as I was, I saw the fun in it too.

"Her Highness is sad 'cause her cookie time got cut short!" I answered cheerfully, spreading my arms wide.

Sirius gave me a defeated look, but he still picked me up like it was nothing. "Then allow me to raise your spirits. Let us head for the rose garden."

Every member of the royal family had a personal "seal" to help distinguish them from one another. Mine was the "red rose," and the "rose garden" was how people referred to the castle garden made in my name.

Guess I'll find out what he's up to soon, I thought as he carried me off.

There were about twenty grand-looking knights standing in a row at the garden. They were all wearing unfamiliar red uniforms. Sirius took me all the way up to them before he lowered me to the ground and performed his own knight's salute.

"Your Highness Princess Serafina, this shall be your personal guard—the Royal Red Shield."

"Oh, wow!" Sirius did tell me that he was going to make a guard force, but I didn't think there would be so many people. "I thought there would only be two more people besides Canopus."

In my opinion, three royal guards were enough to protect me, a single person. When I said as much aloud, Sirius looked at me in exasperation. "Just three? That's not enough to make a unit."

"Nuh-uh! *My* knights would be good enough! I'm glad you're not talking so stuffily anymore, though. Anyway, everyone here looks so strong!"

From what I could see from turning my head around to look at them, everyone was big, burly, and tough-looking—probably because they actually *were* tough. Sirius said himself that he'd put together a team on Canopus's level, and he was true to his word.

It was very nice of him to put in that much effort for me. I leaned in and gave him a hug.

This caused all the knights in the row to jump back, as if they were startled. What was that all about? I was going to turn in their direction, but then Sirius stroked my head and my attention went back to him.

"Do you like them?" he asked, a strong note of pride in his voice.

Sirius took his knighthood very seriously, and he respected fellow knights more than anything. He was showing off his team to me like they were fine treasures.

His feelings were very clear. Plus, I could tell that he had picked out the cream of the crop for me. "Wow, thank you, Sirius! They're all wonderful! But are the Horned Beast Knights going to be okay without them?" I asked, feeling both happy and apologetic at the same time.

In response, Sirius howled in laughter. He really was in a good mood. However, the knights lined up behind him stared at him, stricken, before turning their eyes away as if they'd caught a glimpse of some unspeakable horror.

It was hard to say if Sirius noticed their reaction. "Ha ha ha, you're the one I need to protect the most," he said, sounding amused. "Hence why I picked the best team for the Royal Red Shield. This royal guard might be a stronger force to reckon with than the Horned Beast Knights."

"Oh, wow." I wondered if this was one of his signature bad jokes.

As I tilted my head, Sirius went on. It was hard to tell whether he was joking or serious. "They're the best of the best, and they all have plenty of experience slaying monsters. They can guard you *and* fight alongside you when you're doing your saint work on the battlefield. I'm going with twenty people as a trial run, but I can always add more if need be."

"What? That's already too many! You're joking, right?" I was startled.

But instead of answering me, Sirius started introducing me to a knight—a tall, blond man who looked like he was in his mid-thirties. He stepped forward, a pleasant smile on his face.

"At your service, Princess Serafina. I am Deneb Bonino, captain of the Royal Red Shield."

His smile was so kind, so I happily smiled back. "Nice to meet you, I'm Serafina Náv. Hope we get along!"

Captain Deneb smiled again at my greeting.

The other knights started introducing themselves after that, which meant that I had to learn twenty names all at once... It made me realize how bad my memory was. Well, um, to be fair! Twenty *was* a lot to remember! They all started blending into each other after a while.

As I was grumbling inwardly, I remembered how I still had the cookies I shoved into my pocket. I pulled two of them out and stuffed one into Sirius's mouth. "This is a cookie just for you, Sirius! I bet this will help you memorize stuff."

"Mmf! You're the one who needs the memorization skills, not me... Oh, this is sweet. Not that I'm into sweet things. Ah, yes, come to think of it, I'm sure your brain is working on overdrive because of all this extra stimulation."

"Tee hee hee." I giggled as I munched on the other cookie.

Sirius looked at me in amusement. "Is the captain's name the only one you remember?" he muttered. "If the cookie helps you remember a second name, that'll be double the results."

"Mmm? Whatchu say, Sirimyus?"

"Your pronunciation was so jumbled I didn't quite catch that. Was that my name you said? I was worried that all the new names would push the existing ones out of your memory. Glad you didn't forget me," Sirius said with an amused laugh.

The knights recoiled at the chuckle—which made me wonder why on earth they would do such a thing. Sirius wasn't scary at all. Maybe they were jealous that he got to eat a cookie and they didn't? I only had enough for the two of us today, so I would have to bring enough for everyone next time.

As I sat in Sirius's arms, chewing on my last cookie, I made sure to commit *that* to my memory.

INTERLUDE

The Second Princess's Royal Guard

THE DAY BEFORE Serafina was introduced to her royal guard, every knight stationed in the capital was called to the training hall. Once there, they were told that there would be a guard squad created specifically for the second princess.

For the knights in attendance, this announcement was like a bolt out of the blue. For a moment, murmurs rippled through the hall. The First Knight Brigade already existed for guarding the royals, and they handled everyone—including the king and crown prince. It was clear that, if the second princess was getting a unit all to herself, that meant she was special in some way.

Serafina was indeed special, although that wasn't part of the official announcement. She was born with golden eyes blessed by the Spirit Lord, could understand the spirit language, and, at the tender age of six, she already had a pact with a spirit child.

It was for this reason that Sirius urged the king to create a royal guard force for her, and the king more or less agreed—even he was worried about her standing. It was common knowledge that she'd lived outside the castle until very recently. The king feared that if it ever came to light that she was sent away to a villa because she was born blind, her reputation would suffer deeply. By approving the new squad, he wanted the world to know that she was a beloved member of the family.

Ignorant of these specific circumstances, however, the knights all frowned in bemusement. *"The second princess is only six—not to mention that she lived far outside of the castle for a long time. Does she really deserve special treatment?"* they wondered.

Meanwhile, Kaus Australis—captain of the First Knight Brigade—began announcing the members of the newly formed royal guard.

"Miaplacidus Ames!"

"Yes, sir!"

"Mirach Quark!"

"Yes, sir!"

"Scheat Knowles!"

"Yes, sir!"

The atmosphere in the hall grew ever more strained as the names were called out. Each transferee was an elite member of their respective brigade.

"What? No way," one knight said with a hushed whisper. "Even Scheat? All of the top three of the First Knight Brigade have been transferred!"

"Not just the First Brigade either. They're even poaching elites from the Second Brigade, like Mirach. I don't get it—isn't Her

Highness just a six-year-old? Why does *she* need so many of our best knights?"

As the rumblings grew louder, the First Knight Brigade captain called out the final name. "Deneb Bonino, captain of the Second Knight Brigade!"

At that moment, a stillness seized the hall. One could hear a pin drop in the hush.

The First Knight Brigade captain continued, as if impervious to the silence: "Captain Deneb will be relieved of his current duties and take up a new position as a royal guard captain. That is all."

Every single knight was stunned to hear that even Captain Deneb, an integral part of the knight brigades, would be transferring to the royal guard.

Right then, Vice-Commander Sirius took a step forward. He brushed his gaze over the crowd and said, his face stony as a statue: "I personally selected every transferee."

A jolt of surprise ran through the entire room. There were all sorts of speculations running through the knights' minds: Was there some kind of political machination at play? Did the transferees commit some kind of faux pas and were getting demoted as a result?

But if it was Sirius's decision, then they knew that it had to be above board.

The knights listened attentively as Sirius continued. "Princess Serafina is a saint, and she is the prized jewel of our kingdom! You will support her with that in mind! The work of the royal guard demands the transferees' talents. Whether you were selected for the team or not, I trust that you will dedicate yourself to your duty!"

"Yes, sir!"

Sirius's charisma was magnetic. The knights only needed to know that he was in charge of the decision-making to accept it unconditionally. They knew that there had to be a good reason why so many people were transferred. They were positive that, in time, they would understand the rationale for themselves.

◇ ◇ ◇

And thus, a royal guard was chosen for its lofty task. When the knights actually laid eyes on the second princess, however, they all shared the same thought: "Yep, that's a six-year-old, all right." The only remarkable thing about her appearance was her red hair, a sign that she was favored by the spirits.

The knights once again found themselves at a loss. Why did such a young princess need an elite guard squad? They were convinced that they'd find out the answer once they met her, but even seeing her up close left them as mystified as ever.

The confused knights barely even registered to Serafina. She trotted over to Sirius and gave him a hug as if it was an everyday occurrence.

The knights' eyes boggled at the sight—in their minds, Sirius was an unimpeachable figurehead. How could the princess hug this great man, who they had to muster courage to speak to, so casually?

Instead of chastising the girl, Sirius started patting her on the head. Everyone else was rendered speechless, their eyes transfixed by the surreal sight. The Sirius they knew never gave the time of day to anything other than honing the knights. More to the point, they'd never seen his normally cold eyes light up with such joy.

But here Sirius was, showing unambiguous affection to Princess Serafina. And she spoke to him with remarkable ease, not even bothering to address him by his title. None of the princes nor the other princess had the right to do that. The scene before them made it clear that Serafina occupied a special place in Sirius's heart.

Just then, a cheerful voice rang out.

"Wow, I sure know how to pick 'em!"

It was the kingdom's exalted monarch, who had appeared seemingly out of nowhere.

"Y-Your Majesty!" The knights stiffened in shock before hastily straightening up and performing their salute.

But the king brushed them off with a wave of his hand. "I'm just here to watch Serafina, don't mind me," he responded cheerfully and approached the princess. "Hey, Serafina, Daddy's here! Did you know he picked out these knights just for you? Now that you're seeing them for yourself, what do you think? They're strong enough to look the part, right?"

The king was just trying to curry favor with Serafina in his usual way, but the knights had no way of knowing this.

"What? His Majesty was the one who chose us? The vice-commander made it sound like he personally evaluated our skills for the job. What's the story here?" they muttered to themselves. *"I was expecting something new and exciting when Vice-Commander Sirius said, 'The work of the royal guard demands the transferees' talents,' but it all boils down to guarding the king's beloved daughter... although logically, there's nothing else it* could *be."*

Everyone reached the same conclusion: *"The king and the vice-commander both adore the second princess. That's why they place so much importance on guarding her. This job is pretty cut-and-dried compared to what we usually do."*

Their impressions were only strengthened when Sirius said, "Here is your first mission: Ten days from now, I will be taking Serafina on a vacation to the west coast. I will be staying there for a week, although it may be longer depending on the circumstances."

"What?!" The knights gaped—Sirius had never once taken an extended personal break. It was totally out of character for him to take the princess on a trip to the kingdom's west coast.

Captain Deneb took a step forward out of the throng of astonished knights. "Vice-Commander Sirius, will the First Knight Brigade accompany us to the destination?" he asked with a straight face.

This was the obvious question. This royal guard existed solely to protect Serafina, while the First Knight Brigade typically shielded Sirius.

But Sirius ran a hand through his hair, looking perplexed.

"No, I don't need a guard. While I could protect Serafina all by myself...I am aware that that would be bad form."

He glanced at Captain Deneb's face, but the other man only nodded gravely.

"I'm sure you're baffled about why I would bring so many knights on a vacation," Sirius went on resignedly, "but this is the right opportunity to test our royal guard's efficacy. For Serafina's protection, this team should suffice."

Captain Deneb was silent in the face of Sirius's sharp reply.

Sirius was the vice-commander of the knight brigades and a member of the royal family, making him one of the three most important figures in the entire kingdom. He was in no position to casually offer himself up as a bodyguard, but here he was, trying to serve as a mere knight without showing a sliver of awareness of his own status.

As concerning as this was, Sirius *was* the strongest in the brigade, so nobody had it in them to reproach him. Even so, the First Knight Brigade still had to do its job. Captain Deneb thought it would be deeply unwise for them *not* to come along.

"I will make sure the entire royal guard attends for protection and so they get acclimated to the job," he said.

Inwardly, he added: *"And I'll pass this information along to the First Knight Brigade so that I can get at least a few of their knights to come."*

Either way, Captain Deneb expected that this initial job of protecting the princess on her vacation was a sign of things to come. This was a perturbing thought, for their royal guard consisted entirely of knights who fought on the front lines. Compared to their previous exploits, this job seemed unchallenging—boring, even.

"I just have to get them to adjust their expectations."

There would probably never be another dream team on this level. Assembling a group of such formidable knights was bound to cause its share of trouble, but he wanted to earn the respect of his comrades through their joint toils. Hopefully, there would be a chance for the knights to cultivate their skills.

"I can only hope that happens, at least."

Deneb prayed for the best.

◇ ◇ ◇

As it turned out, his optimistic prediction for the newly established royal guard appeared to be spot-on. The knights did not complain about their lot, got along without too much fuss, and accepted that they were part of a team.

This was because every member was a professional through and through. To put it bluntly: Even if they were dissatisfied on the inside, nobody was going to show it outwardly. On top of this, Serafina stoked their protective urges. Because of her many sheltered years in the villa, her existence seemed both novel and precarious. Everyone actively took charge in guarding her, and nobody wanted to show discontent in front of her.

The royal guard worked extremely well together, but there were two knights in particular (Canopus notwithstanding) who went above and beyond for Serafina.

The first was Scheat Knowles, the third-ranked member of the First Knight Brigade. Even beyond his tall and brawny physique, he had a rather eye-catching appearance: The right side of his head was covered with red hair, while the left side was blond. Although he was a free-spirited individual at heart, his rigorous duty demanded that he suppress that part of his personality. Everyone knew him as a serious man of few words.

Just three days after his transfer, however, he began letting his true self shine through. That day, when stationed in the rear garden for the afternoon shift, he called out to Serafina in a cheerful tone. This side of him was completely alien to the other squad members.

"Princess Serafina, are you picking flowers in the weed garden again? The sunlight is strong in the afternoon—anything you pick is going to wither right away in the basket. Want me to bring you a bucket of water?"

"Nah, it's okay!" Serafina refused. "They're not for display."

The strong and hale Canopus was going through a rare bout of sickness, so Serafina was planning to use herbs for a healing potion. It would have been quicker to cast magic, but despite his significant ails, Canopus insisted that no one enter his room for fear of spreading the illness.

Upon hearing what Serafina said, Scheat pulled some herbs out of the basket. "If you're not displaying them, are you planning on having them as a late-night snack? The lady knights are always talking about how grass is good for your health, but I've never resorted to eating it before."

The crouching Serafina gazed up at Scheat, trying to work out how best to explain herself. The moment her eyes fell on him, however, they widened in surprise. "Oh, Scheat! Why aren't you wearing a shirt? Did you lose your uniform?"

"Ha ha ha, not in the least! I'm just gearing up for our beach trip in a week. Vice-Commander Sirius said to go in our own clothes instead of our uniforms. Pretty obvious when you think about it, right? We'd practically be shouting that you're a VIP if you've got two dozen knights around you."

Serafina nodded deeply at this. "Oh! You have a point."

"A light shirt would work for the beach, but since I'm always buttoned up in my uniform, you'd be able to see how my skin's really pale underneath. Your Highness, did you know that different places can have massively different standards for people? The knight brigades love strong folk, but at the beach, it's all about how tan you are!"

"Oh, really?!" Serafina's eyes widened. Her expression screamed, "I had no idea!"

Seeing this, Scheat decided to respond with an exaggerated flourish. He scrunched up his face like he was trying to withstand a terrible burden and covered his eyes with his hand...although it just looked like he was being blinded by the sun.

"Indeed! And as your faithful knight, I could not possibly let my body bring you shame! I'm making the best use of today's sunlight!" he said, bringing his hand away from his eyes to reveal a guileless smile.

Upon closer inspection, Scheat was not just shirtless—his pants were rolled up above his knees, and his feet were bare. By all appearances, he was not merely "opening up" as a person, he was letting himself go entirely in order to amuse the sparkly-eyed Serafina.

"Sch-Scheat! Why are you half-naked?!"

"This is hardly an appropriate sight for Her Highness!"

His fellow knights were late to the scene. When they saw Scheat in his state of undress, they shouted in astonishment...

Only for Serafina to rebuke them with an enraptured look on her face. "You don't get it! Tanned people are the strongest at the beach! Scheat is just trying to power up as a knight!"

"Huh? What?"

"Sch-Scheat! What lies have you been telling sweet Princess Serafina?!"

As the two knights grilled Scheat, Serafina spoke up cheerfully. "Tee hee hee! The sun is strong today—great for getting a tan. Why don't you two try soaking up some sun too?"

"No, uh, we, um..." the knights said weakly. "I, uh, doubt that we could protect you without, uh..."

Scheat seized his chance. "As you can see from looking at me, the knights are totally pale below the neck. Tan lines are a terrible look at the beach!" he said assuredly.

For a moment, the two knights looked as if they were almost convinced by Scheat's argument, but they quickly returned to their senses. "N-no, we're fine," they insisted. "We'll get a natural tan after two or three days."

Scheat folded his arms and shook his head in clear disagreement. "That's the thing. You guys are super macho. The tan lines pretty much out you all as knights who are trapped in their uniforms all day. The vice-commander told us to wear our own clothes to hide our identities, and you're gonna ruin that by exposing your pale asses?"

The knights jumped, as if struck by lightning.

Evidently, Scheat's argument must have worked, because five minutes later there was an assembly of half-naked knights in the castle's rear garden.

This was the point where the *other* knight who doted on Serafina appeared on the scene.

His name was Mirach Quark, second-ranked member of the Second Knight Brigade. A slender, baby-faced young man with light-pink hair, he had a saccharine air of boyishness around him. At the same time, he was caring to the extreme. Most of the knights were quite gruff, so he was known among his comrades as the "mother hen" for tending to Serafina's needs with tact and an eye for detail.

(Incidentally, the knights mentally referred to Sirius as "the Ultimate Mother Hen." This was the royal guard's most tightly kept secret, however, and nobody uttered this moniker aloud unless they were drunk.)

Mirach was in the process of bringing Serafina one of her red ribbons that she had requested when he happened upon the half-naked, barefoot knights. This throng of clothing-deficient individuals stood around the princess as she picked grass and sang a cheerful little ditty.

An ominous scowl crossed his face, and his hand went to the sword at his hip.

"H-hold your horses, Mirach! We're just sunbathing! Look, even our fingers are pale! Only knights who wear gloves would be this buff and pasty. We're simply trying to erase any trace of our occupations so that the princess can enjoy her trip incognito!" Scheat waggled his finger, flustered. He knew that, contrary to his appearance, Mirach was a short-tempered soul.

But Mirach narrowed his eyes. "Oh, is *that* what's going on here? And here I thought you lot were wicked monsters masquerading as knights. Or perhaps some manner of spell made you erroneously believe that the castle garden is a bathhouse. Either way, it's unseemly for Princess Serafina's eyes. The trash must be disposed of," he said in a hard tone as he pulled his sword slightly out of his scabbard.

Scheat's voice raised in alarm. "C-calm down, Mirach! It might look weird to you, but being a knight isn't all about wearing the uniform! We're doing this for Princess Serafina!"

Unfortunately for him, Mirach's raised eyebrow showed he wasn't being swayed by the argument one bit. "Scheat, how about you put a stop to this ludicrousness? We're going to a private

beach exclusively for the royal family. As proud as I'm sure you are of your body, nobody but the knights are going to see it. Besides, the tan lines will disappear after a few days at the shore."

"What?!" Serafina, who had been listening behind them, let out a cry of surprise.

Scheat smiled to reassure her before turning back to Mirach with a scowl. "Mirach, you're just talking about the best-case scenario! Things pretty much never go according to plan. I took charge *in case* things go awry!"

Upon hearing these words, Serafina's expression changed from one of astonishment to deep admiration. "Oh, wow, Scheat! That was such a cool thing to say! 'I took charge'—remind me to use that line myself!"

"Princess Serafina..."

Mirach grimaced at his woefully naive charge...and immediately threw a sharp glare in Scheat's direction.

At twenty-three, Mirach was one year Scheat's senior. He saw it as his role to rein in Scheat's free-wheeling tendencies, and today was no exception.

It was pretty amusing from an onlooker's perspective to watch the slender and baby-faced Mirach tell off the tall and muscular Scheat. Everyone left and let the two of them have at it. Mirach's reprimanding voice rang out in the rear garden for quite a while after that.

One man watched this commotion silently from afar: Captain Deneb, leader of the royal guard.

None of the other knights had noticed their captain's presence. When Deneb caught sight of them milling around the princess without their shirts on, he was tempted to yell at them, but he willfully suppressed the urge and kept watch for a while.

When he saw Serafina smiling brightly, he silently turned away. As secluded as the rear garden was, it was a big problem for the knights to strip in front of their charge—hence his desire to scold them—but when he did exactly that in the previous days, Serafina had been gloomy and tearful.

"C-Captain Deneb, the knights were only naughty because I let them be."

He suspected that if he went out and rebuked the knights, Serafina would see it as a criticism against her for letting them go half-naked. She would be crestfallen.

"Princess Serafina's got a big heart, eh? Plus, I gotta remember that she's a kid who doesn't have anyone her own age to play with. The knights could be filling that role in her life. When I think of it that way, I suppose I can give them some leeway as long as they get the guarding part right," Captain Deneb told himself.

Inwardly, though, he was still in turmoil. *Is 'some' leeway the right way of putting it? Toplessness is a no-go, right? Right?! Aaaargh!*

He sighed heavily.

"Either way, I wouldn't want to deprive Princess Serafina of her chance to have fun," he muttered. "Besides, I suppose I should be thanking her for how well the knights have been getting along. I thought for sure there would be egos butting heads in such an elite team, but they're all in this for Princess Serafina. Guess I'll look the other way this time."

The young princess brought a joyful smile to any occasion, which was apparently enough to catch the knights by surprise and rid them of any desire to make serious trouble.

On the flip side, they *were* getting into constant childish spats. This was not, perhaps, the greatest of looks for a squad of elite knights.

"But still, I have to wonder...why on earth did Vice-Commander Sirius go out of his way to pick *these* members for her royal guard?" Captain Deneb muttered the question that had been swirling in his mind ever since he heard of the team's formation. "They're overqualified, no matter how you slice it."

At the time, he was disappointed that he still couldn't understand what was going through Vice-Commander Sirius's head, even after fighting alongside each other for so long...but when he eventually did come to learn why the finest knights were assembled, he would look back fondly on these days as a period of blissful ignorance.

A Tale of the Secret Saint ZERO

POINT OF VIEW
CANOPUS

Master Healer Serafina and Her Ailing Personal Knight

"OPEN UUUUP, Canopus!"

Knock knock! The rapping on my dorm room door was accompanied by an adorable voice. As soon as I figured out who it was, I sat up in my bed.

"My word...Princess Serafina! This is no place for you to be!" I cried as loudly as I could muster. "Please leave at once, I beg of you."

"Oh, Canopus, your throat sounds terrible! Let me iiiiin! I'll heal you up!"

Knock knock!

I simply couldn't let Princess Serafina keep pounding away. I rose out of bed and headed for the door, but even just that slight amount of exertion was enough to drain me. As I clung to the doorknob, I lamented the frailness of my body.

"Princess Serafina, you needn't trouble yourself over my ailments. I contracted this condition from my dorm mates, so I know how it will play out. I will have a fever for three days, and then I will be back to normal. More importantly, I do not wish to spread it to you. I urge you to stay far from my room."

Despite my plaintive pleas, my magnanimous liege knocked on the door again.

"I won't get sick, Canopus. I'm a saint, remember? Besides, I only wanna be in your room for a tiiiiiny bit so I can heal you. Pleaaaase?"

Princess Serafina once told me that she had a pact with a spirit child. I had never actually seen this spirit for myself, however, nor had she ever wielded her saint powers before me. Thus, I must regrettably admit that a part of me thought that her abilities were slight. Of course, the fact that she already had a pact at the age of six was a sure indication of her talents—even if she was still learning, she could certainly call herself a saint without fear—but without seeing her skills for myself, I could not take her claims at face value and allow her inside.

I knelt at the door and bowed my head deeply. "I am so truly grateful for your concern. However, my duty is to protect you. I cannot allow you near me while I am ill. Please forgive me...*ack!* Mmfh! Ahem!"

I must have strained my throat from speaking too much, for I broke out into a coughing fit at the end.

I cursed myself for my blunder, but ironically, my indiscretion appeared to touch Princess Serafina's heart. She hurriedly backed away from the door. "Wh-what an awful cough you have, Canopus! I'm so sorry, I didn't mean to push you. I won't try to use magic on you anymore, so just get some rest, okay?!"

With those panicked words, Her Highness trotted away down the hallway. This was accompanied by the sounds of several other footsteps: the knights of the royal guard. I breathed a sigh of relief.

I staggered back to my bed and collapsed on it. Sleep would envelop me soon, I suspected. I would feel better the next time I woke up, and I only needed to repeat this pattern for three days...

Or so I assumed.

That afternoon, a fellow knight came to visit me. It was Scheat, a brawny fellow with red and golden hair. He barged right in and shook me awake.

"Hey, Canopus. You look like crap. It's good to get some sleep, but you should drink some water whenever you wake up. Should be enough for you to pull through," he said as he slammed a large jug on my bedside table. It was filled with water—a clear indication that he came out of concern for my health.

"Thanks, and sorry," I said. "It will take me three days to heal. Take care of Princess Serafina in my stead."

Scheat folded his arms and cocked an amused brow. "Oh? She's our liege too, so I get where you're coming from, but I reckon you're special to her," he said as he pulled out a little bottle with a red ribbon on it. "She picked herbs and made her own healing potion this afternoon. Said she wanted you to get better straight away. Plus, she wrapped her ribbon around the bottle as a get-well-soon gift. Anyway, drink up."

He plopped the bottle into my hand.

As I peered at it in confusion, his voice fell on my ears. "Take it now. Her Highness ordered me to make sure you guzzled every last drop. Give it back to me when you're done, so I can give it to her as proof. Oh, and one more thing. We expect you back at work in two days, not three. Make sure you give all the credit to Princess Serafina's medicine."

"Scheat..."

"Don't worry, everyone will back you up when you return. You just have to show up."

Only a scant few days had passed since Scheat was assigned to Princess Serafina's care, yet he already cared deeply about her feelings. I was glad to see it.

I opened the bottle and gulped down its contents. The potion had a sweet scent, and I could not help but grimace when it fell on my tongue. The taste was far more syrupy than any healing potion I'd ever had before, almost unbelievably so.

Scheat saw my face and asked, "Taste funny?"

"It's like no other healing potion I've ever encountered. This is like drinking honey," I answered frankly.

Scheat put a hand to his brow. "You're right on the money. Our princess mixed some honey into it for good measure."

"She did?"

I was no expert on healing potions, but I'd never heard of honey as an ingredient.

Scheat cast a sideways glance at my bemused face. "Canopus, don't blame her for getting an ingredient or two wrong. She said the honey is to soothe your cough, so she went out of her way to get it for you. Think of it as her way of showing consideration."

"To think she went to such lengths..." I muttered, feeling greatly touched.

This caused Scheat to wave his hands in an exaggerated manner and launch into a lecture. "You don't realize how much our princess loves you! Let me fill you in. She took *ages* making that potion, adding in special extra flourishes—and not just the honey either. She even tossed in these pink flowers to make it smell nice and used this sweet-looking red fruit for the taste."

"I'm happy to hear it." I paused, and then said, "Although I'm not terribly familiar with medicines, I did take a class on the basics. I remember them saying that the most important thing for making potions was to combine the right ingredients in the right proportions. Was it wise for Princess Serafina to mix a variety of components in an ad hoc manner?"

I asked this question out of pure and simple curiosity, only for Scheat to scowl and slap me on the back. "Canopus, knights aren't supposed to sweat the small stuff! Illness is all in the mind, as they say. You'll get better as long as you think you will."

"True enough." I nodded, because that was more or less my line of thinking as well.

"Let me just add that our princess spent a long while singing, dancing, and pacing around the medicine. I'm pretty sure one of her lines was 'Pain, pain, go away! Leave Canopus alone today!' or something like that."

Scheat spread his arms wide and lifted one of his legs as far as it could go.

For a long moment, I said nothing. I wondered if perhaps he was copying what Princess Serafina did for me.

"You get it now?! Our princess put her heart and soul in that medicine! It's slow-acting according to her... She didn't say exactly how long it would take. Just act like you're feeling a little better come tomorrow morning, then make your return in two days, not three. Doesn't matter if you're fully healed!"

And so, through no input of my own, the date of my recovery was decided... Yet for some reason, I realized as soon as Scheat was out the door that I was, in fact, feeling totally fine.

"I'm cured? Impossible! And yet..."

Mere moments ago, my body had been flushed with fever, but now it was back to normal. The pain in my head and joints had also dissipated. I put a hand to my throat and noticed that the pain was absent there as well.

"Princess Serafina's medicine worked..."

Of that, there was not a shadow of doubt in my mind—for it was the act of drinking my liege's healing potion that brought about this recovery.

I was both awed by Princess Serafina's prowess as a saint and deeply moved by the kindness in her heart. This affliction would have been over in just three days of misery, and yet she took the time to make a healing potion for me...a mere knight.

"My liege is truly a wonderful soul."

Not for the first time, I thanked the stars for allowing me to serve someone so benevolent.

The next day, I returned to work, fully restored.

Scheat looked at me as if I had grown another head. "You're overdoing it, Canopus!" he said, running up to me with evident concern on his face. "You could've waited till tomorrow."

I informed him briskly of my good health. "Princess Serafina's potion worked wonders."

Scheat shook his head in astonishment. "Wow, Canopus! You're even more dedicated than I realized! But hey, I can't hate guys like you. Anytime you need someone to pick up the slack for you today, you can count on me!" he declared without a hint of ill will.

Scheat seemed skeptical that a healing potion with unconventional ingredients would work. I suppose that it *was* hard to believe that my body had recovered without putting it to the test.

When I looked at him, he smiled back at me. Inwardly, I marveled that I was not only blessed with a good master but faithful comrades as well.

"Oh? I'll take you up on that, then," I said.

"Sure thing. It's no skin off my teeth!" said Scheat, before he ran off to inform Princess Serafina about my condition.

The other knights noticed my presence shortly afterward.

"Canopus! Are you feeling better?" Mirach looked happy for me.

"Good for you!" Miaplacidus called out to me next, his expression similarly merry.

In the distance, I saw Scheat speaking to Princess Serafina. She swung her head around to peer at me, her eyes sparkling.

"Oh yippee, Canopus! You're all better!" my liege declared with a sunny smile.

The sky behind her was just as dazzling—an ocean of pure blue.

It suddenly occurred to me that this beauty was perhaps a glimpse of her world, or at least what her world *should* be.

And in my heart, I vowed once more that it would stay that way.

POINT OF VIEW

SIRIUS

Playing Tag With Serafina

"CHILDREN ARE SURPRISINGLY perceptive," someone once told me, although I don't remember who.

As I gazed down at the scene outside the window, a dull ache ran through my head.

Serafina was playing with the knights. That in itself was fine; it was important for children to stay active, and one could say that the knights were fortunate to have some respite in their busy schedules.

However.

"Fine" didn't quite describe the game they were playing.

At first glance, it appeared to be tag. The one difference was that when the person who was "it" touched another participant, that person would pose and freeze. As the game progressed, more and more people would be stuck in a pose.

Out of simple curiosity, I tried to work out what pose they were doing. I'd witnessed this game on numerous occasions, you see. Last time, everyone did banana poses, and the time before that, they were squids.

This time, however, each knight struck a different pose.

At first, I thought they were holding the position they were in when they got caught, but that did not appear to be the case upon further inspection. This led me to think that they were operating under some kind of theme, although I could not work out what exactly it was.

As I peered down at the scene, stroking my chin in thought, one of the knights raised a hand to his torso—a knight's pose. So they were emulating knights? Was everyone supposed to do their signature move?

Then I noticed another knight cross his arms imperiously. Someone else thrust his arm in front of himself as if he was rejecting something. Knight poses were out of the equation, then. What occupation *were* they doing?

The man next to him lifted one leg in the air and held that position. I had to say that he had a good sense of balance. Then the knight next to him sat on the ground, crossed his legs, and pretended as if he were drinking something as he ran a hand through his hair.

Okay, what on earth was *that*?

It was frustrating how the answer eluded me just when I thought I'd had it. I gave the question some serious thought, bearing in mind that this was a children's game.

The fellow who just got tagged looked as if he was petting something. What was he doing? I didn't have the foggiest idea. There was no rhyme or reason to the poses.

As I crossed my arms and frowned down at the scene, Serafina was tagged. She chose to pose as a squid. She lifted her leg, and...

Even through the closed window, I could hear the knights roaring in laughter. It was at that moment when it finally occurred to me what they were copying.

"Oh, now I see it. They've all got some nerve. Here I come," I muttered darkly as I headed for the door, sword in hand.

Damn those fools. They'd pay for my headache.

I reached the garden just as the person who was "it" caught the last participant. The knight reached a hand out with a bored expression and held that pose.

"What are you copying?" I asked him from behind, projecting my voice louder than usual.

The knight who was "it" jumped in horror at the sight of me, although the knight I spoke to appeared not to notice my presence.

"I'm being the vice-commander when the prettiest lady in the secretariat gave him the 'Most Handsome Member of the Horned Beast Knights' medal for the third year straight," he answered cheerfully, without turning around. "Ha ha ha, I was there! The vice-commander looked soooo done with it all! Hot guys sure are a different breed!"

At that moment, several other knights twitched, having noticed me. "None of you move a muscle!" I barked.

My voice alerted everyone at the scene to my presence. They froze.

"Oh, so you *can* stand still when you put your mind to it. I noticed that many of you were shaking when you were trying to hold your poses. It made me fear that you needed to retrain your core muscles," I said as I clapped a hand on the shoulder of the knight in front of me.

"Yikes!"

"Now then, you said the words 'hot guy' just now. I don't quite understand what you meant by that. I have to say that your choice of words bothers me. I want a report on this 'hot guy' before the end of today!"

"Y-y-y-yes, sir!" My subordinate nodded meekly.

I went to Serafina next. She was still holding her adorable squid pose.

"Clever Serafina, your squid impression was impeccable." I stroked her head. "I can see how you've got your leg raised. It reminds me of the pose you thought up for me when you demanded...er, asked...me to emulate a squid not too long ago. You said I was a 'special silver squid,' if I recall. That was a key clue. Thanks to you, I was able to figure out that everyone was attempting to mimic me."

A smattering of groans greeted my deductions.

"Argh!" yelled one knight.

"Urgh!" grunted another.

"That's it, I'm dead. I had a good run, boys. Thanks for the memories!"

As all of this went on, Serafina relaxed her stance and beamed up at me. "Was I good at doing your squid pose?"

"Yes, very. Everything you do is adorable."

"Eh heh heh heh." Serafina giggled happily.

I patted her head one more time before turning my attention to the knight standing next to her. He was the only one beyond reproach.

"Not a bad knight pose," I said to Mirach.

"Thank you very much," he responded with a straight face.

I then faced the knight next to Mirach. "Okay, so you've got your arms folded imperiously. You think that's something I would do?"

"Er, um, no, of course not! It's an artistic abstraction! I know you don't *actually* do the hoity-toity thing, it's just the way it looks to us."

"Speak for yourself!" A torrent of dissenting voices immediately spoke up.

"Don't betray me like this!" the panicking knight insisted. "You were all cracking up just a moment ago!"

I smiled thinly at him and handed down my sentence. "You demonstrated a very poor understanding of me. You're to submit a report too! I want a detailed explanation of how the discrepancy between your 'artistic abstraction' and how I actually am came about!"

The knight sniffled, crestfallen. "Yes, sir!"

I paid no heed to the knight as he collapsed to the ground. My next subject of attention was the knight who had his hand thrust in front of him as if he was rejecting something. "Care to explain that pose?"

The knight said nothing.

"Did you not hear my question?" I intoned as I kicked the bricks surrounding the flowerbed near my feet.

The knight's gaze went straight to the ground. "It's, um, you when you refused a young lady's gift," he said mutedly.

"What?!" Serafina's startled voice sounded behind me. "Sirius has refused presents before?!"

My first impulse was to be defensive, but I mustered a response for her edification. "Yes, if I'm not on familiar terms with the other person. Listen, Serafina, you also mustn't accept gifts from people who aren't me or your immediate family."

"Okay!" Serafina nodded earnestly.

I shifted my gaze back to the knight in front of me. "Out of all the poses I've ever done, you chose one of me rejecting a lady. That's the issue here. I want a report about your decision-making process!"

The knight trembled. "Y-yes, sir!"

My next port of call was the knight with good balance, who still had one leg raised. "What's that pose?"

"Sir! Much like how you kicked those bricks just now, this pose is of you kicking a desk when you're cowing a knight into submission!"

"I expect a report about *your* decision-making process as well!"

The next person in line was a difficult one to figure out. Scheat was sitting on the ground with his legs crossed, running a hand through his hair as he was pretending to drink something. "What's the story behind this one?"

"Sir! This is you when you're sitting on a sofa, drinking wine as you do a cool flourish with your hair!"

"Have you ever seen me do this?"

"I have not, sir, but it's the picture on the cover of bestselling book *An Elegant Day in the Life of the Handsome Chief Duke*!"

Right. The "chief duke" of this country was me, Duke Ulysses. So there was a book with that kind of title in circulation, hm?

"Bring that book to me tomorrow! And a report on why you chose to reference that cover!"

Finally, I stopped in front of Miaplacidus, who was frozen in the middle of petting something in the air. "What are *you* doing?"

"Sir! This is you in a gown after you get out of the bath. You are petting something soft and fluffy on your knee—as depicted in another illustration in *An Elegant Day in the Life of the Handsome Chief Duke*!"

"Okay, you bring me a copy too! And a report like Scheat's!"

Well, this was disconcerting. As I contemplated banning this book within the knight brigades and confiscating every copy, Serafina tugged on my sleeve. "Sirius, did you come here to check out the 'Sirius Tag' game we were playing 'cause it looked fun? Oh, did you want to join in?"

It took me a while to think of a response to that. "Well, maybe in another hundred years."

"Huh?" Serafina looked up at me quizzically.

I patted her head. "You watch me so closely, Serafina. I understand now what they mean when they say 'children are surprisingly perceptive.' Meanwhile, the adults have been doing 'artistic abstractions' and poses that are completely out of character for me. All I can do is shake my head."

Behind me, the knights who had been tasked with report-writing started commiserating.

"Aww man, it's over for me!" Scheat's voice rang out. "Tell my wife at home that I was a brave man to the very end."

"Impossible," Miaplacidus retorted without missing a beat. "You're single! You don't even have a wife to tell! Anyway, someone pass along these flowers to my daughter. I want her to know that the flowers I saw on my last day reminded me of her smile."

"Talk about a tall order!" Scheat shot back at the dejected Miaplacidus. "You've never even had a girlfriend before, let alone married a woman. So what's this about a daughter? Absolute crazy talk."

As fellow First Knight Brigade expats, Scheat and Miaplacidus had a good rapport. Everyone else appeared to be engaging in pleasant banter as well. I considered making them do laps on top of their reports, but Serafina seemed to enjoy listening to them, so I kept my mouth shut.

Fine, then. They were off the hook today out of consideration for Serafina.

"I'll look after Serafina for today. Now get to work on those reports!"

"Yes, Vice-Commander!"

The knights performed excellent salutes before sprinting off into the distance.

As I watched them go out of the corner of my eye, I said to Serafina, "It's about time for dinner. Time to wash our hands and head to the banquet hall."

"Yep! But you know, Sirius, all the knights love you! It was our first time playing 'Sirius Tag,' but everyone decided straight away what pose they would do! Seems like they all pay a lot of attention to you."

At least two of the knights copied poses from a book about me, but I didn't think it was worth mentioning this aloud.

"Hm. If they've got their eye on me, then I'd best be careful about my conduct," I said to Serafina as we walked to the banquet hall together.

The next morning, I got a headache all over again from reading the knights' reports. Their arguments were absolutely terrible. It seemed clear that whipping their minds into shape was going to take just as much work as Serafina's education.

A Tale of the Secret Saint ZERO

Serafina's Exciting West Coast Trip

IT WAS A LOVELY summer day when my royal guard, led by Sirius, arrived at the west coast.

Since the Náv Kingdom was on the west side of the continent, the "west coast" took up the nation's entire west side. Specifically, we went to the Set Coast due west of the royal capital. My family had a villa there, and the nearby beaches were privately owned.

By the way, though I brought Seven along with me, I gave up on bringing the black fenrir. I thought about painting him a different color and pretending he was a normal dog, but I got the feeling that Sirius would get super mad if he found out. Besides, I was pretending that I hadn't even noticed him living in the garden, so we were better off not being seen together.

When I asked the black fenrir to be a good boy and stay home, he licked my face as if he was saying yes. This took a load off my mind. "I'll bring you a souvenir, okay?" I promised him and then left the castle behind me.

"Let's head for the beach, Your Highness!" Scheat called out to me as I stood in a daze outside the villa.

The knight was already dressed in swim trunks and a shirt with a colorful design. The buttons were all undone, though, showing off his magnificent tan. He also had a purple pendant around his neck, plus matching leather straps around his arms.

Scheat had an eye-catching hair style and striking facial features, so the ladies-in-waiting often said he looked like a "playboy" behind his back. Between his face and current outfit...

"Oh, Scheat! You look like that man in the picture book from the other day! The one who hoodwinks ladies!" I exclaimed, remembering how the fellow in the book had a gaudy shirt and accessories too.

Scheat scowled as if he didn't like what I said. "Don't give me that—I'd never do such a thing!" he insisted. "Behold these abs! Do you know how much time I spend honing these beautiful muscles?! I've been cultivating my abs ever since I joined the knight brigades. No time for anything else."

"O-oh, yeah," I agreed with him, but the sour look on his face told me that I'd said the wrong thing. Maybe I should have said he had wonderful muscles.

I was still feeling bad when Mirach joined the conversation. "Princess Serafina, there's no need to humor Scheat's idiocy. How about changing into your swimwear, seeing as we're at the beach and all?"

I turned around and saw that he was already wearing a long-sleeved swimsuit with shorts over the top.

Wow, when did he get changed? As I gazed around in surprise, I saw that all the knights were in their swimwear too. They wore their uniforms on the way to the villa, so it was only natural for them to switch to beachwear now that they were here, but the colors and patterns were pretty tacky. Plus, it didn't look like they were wearing *enough* clothes.

I couldn't help but think that maybe they were trying a little *too* hard. "Umm, do you all normally wear stuff like that?" I asked timidly.

"No way! We usually wear dark colors. But Scheat told us off, saying, 'You look too plain! Are you *trying* to bring shame on Her Highness?!' We all thought he made a good point, so we went to Scheat's favorite clothing store."

"The shopkeeper recommended this outfit!"

"*And* they told us how to style it!"

"O-oh, really?" To me, it just looked sloppy and not like something any reasonable person would wear, but maybe this was what people wore at the beach.

Then I spied Canopus. Although he was wearing an appropriate outfit for the seaside, he was the odd one out.

"Are your clothes from Sutherland?" I asked, since I knew that Canopus's homeland was a seaside area to the south. "The colors are different from what I'm used to."

I'd never seen an outfit like his before, but it looked good.

"I went shopping with the others, but the trends didn't suit me. I feared that I wouldn't suit the look, so I brought the clothes I was used to," he said, confirming my assumption.

"You have good taste! It looks really nice on you." I clapped my hands.

Canopus's face turned red at my praise. "Thank you very much," he said.

My personal knight was a shy fellow, apparently.

After that, the ladies-in-waiting guided me to my bedroom for the trip, where they dressed me in a frilly one-piece swimsuit and a hooded jacket. When I left the room, my eyes caught sight of Sirius, who was leaning against the wall.

"That outfit is very flattering, Serafina. You look like a flower spirit."

"Thanks, Sirius!" I gave him a hug—it was nice to hear his praise.

Like the other knights, Sirius was wearing a shirt and shorts, but it looked like high-quality stuff, made with crisp white fabric and covered in a blue-and-gold pattern.

He looked nice. *If only the other knights wore tasteful clothes*, I thought. But when I suggested this to Scheat, he narrowed his eyes.

"The vice-commander ordered his clothes from the royal family's tailor. It might look like what we're wearing, but the materials are completely different. Those fancy-schmancy shirts and shorts would eat up half my salary."

"Oh goodness." I giggled at Scheat's joke, but none of the other knights were laughing. That made me look up at Sirius in surprise. "Wait, is Scheat telling the truth? Are you a big spender, Sirius?"

Sirius scowled and picked me up. "Of course he's joking. No one's got a bigger gap between their income and their expenditure than I do."

Though he said the second part in a joking way, it made me wonder if Scheat really was telling the truth. When I looked back over my shoulder at Scheat, he shook his head lightly. "His income is just *that* high."

Sirius must have heard Scheat's grumblings because he shot a glare at the other knight.

"Yikes! I, uh, I'm just envious, is all. Y-y'know...?" Scheat squeaked, sounding rattled. I didn't really get what he was talking about.

Sirius ignored Scheat as he wordlessly stepped out of the villa. Canopus followed after him, and then the other knights hurriedly tagged along.

The moment I was outside, my close companion Seven (who had cast an invisibility spell on himself like usual to stop anyone besides me from being able to see him) scanned our surroundings with sparkling eyes. His gaze quickly settled on a single point. *"I'm gonna take a quick nap,"* he chirped, before diving into a hammock nestled between two trees. Once settled, he soon slumped over with a slovenly look on his face.

"Oh gosh! There are so many things to do at the beach! And it took so much effort to get here," I muttered in exasperation.

How had he immediately fixated on the hammock? Was he really just going to spend the whole trip napping?

"Has your cheeky spirit decided to drop out?" Sirius asked wryly. "We haven't even been in the water yet."

He lifted me higher than usual and propped me on his shoulders.

"Serafina, can you see the ocean?" he asked as he faced west.

"Yep! It's so big and pretty!" I gasped at the sight that came into view.

Pure white sands and a sparkling blue sea danced in my vision. It was such a beautiful scene.

For a while, I sat there entranced by the magnificent view, but when I looked closer, an interesting area between the white and blue caught my eye. White sands surrounded the sea in a crescent shape, and the area was peppered with hundreds of massive rocks.

"Those are fragments of the Lodrigone Continent," Sirius explained when he noticed that my eyes were fixed on the big rocks.

That didn't clear things up for me, though. "What? Didn't the Lodrigone Continent exist a long, long time ago?" I asked, remembering what my tutor had taught me.

Sirius nodded. "Yes. It's the world's oldest continent, said to exist before the dawn of humankind. Over a long course of time, the continent split into smaller fragments and got swallowed by the sea, but the fragments still remain. In other words, those big rocks you see were once a part of the Lodrigone Continent...or so they say. It's why this area has always been under the royal family's strict jurisdiction."

This talk of an ancient continent made me think, *Wow! Those rocks must be pretty mysterious!* But the more I listened to Sirius, the more I got the impression that this applied to the beach as a whole. This area was known as "The Golden Sea" because of the glimmering golden shells that occasionally washed ashore. People said that the shells belonged to the Sea Lord, so it was bad luck to take them away from the shore.

"Oh, the seashells! We gotta pick them all up and put them back into the ocean," I said, leaning forward.

Sirius laughed as he set me down on the sand. "Ha ha ha, I heard they're scarce."

He looked like he was having fun, so I yelled out, "Race you to the ocean!" and sprinted straight for the water.

It was my first time running on sand, and my feet sank right into it making it harder to run than usual. I figured it was time to get serious.

"Serafina Dash!"

I showed off the sprint I reserved for special occasions, but Scheat appeared on my right, keeping up with my stride without breaking a sweat. "You're a fast one, Serafina!" he praised.

"Huh?" I was planning to leave him in the dust. Was I not so fast after all?

Then there was a voice to my left. "Please watch your step, Your Highness!" Even Mirach was keeping up with me.

Hearing rustling behind me, I looked over my shoulder and saw Canopus tailing right behind me. "Princess Serafina, watch where you're going!"

His warning came a little too late, because right then my foot got stuck in the sand. I thought I was going to trip, but he caught me before I hit the ground.

"Th-thank you, Canopus."

Phew! As I was thanking my personal knight, Sirius came striding up next to me. "Hello there, Serafina. Normally, I'd ask, 'Are you okay?' but since we're in a race, I'll be running ahead. Hope you don't mind."

What was I supposed to do about *that*? I quickly wriggled out of Canopus's arms and started running again. "Wait up! *Sirius!*"

We were incredibly close to the sea. I chased Sirius with all I had, but he just laughed and didn't speed up at all.

Thanks to that, I won the race.

"Whoopee! I won! Heh heh heh, good thing I'm a tortoise. You're the hare who lost!"

When I declared my victory, waggling my finger at Sirius, the other knights cocked their heads.

"Princess Serafina is the tortoise?"

"And Vice-Commander Sirius is the hare?" They blanched. "No way, he's a total carnivore! He'd never be a hare!"

They didn't seem to know about the story of the persistent tortoise and the flighty hare. I couldn't be bothered explaining, so I just said, "Sirius is cute as a bunny." This earned me a bunch of scowls, including from Sirius himself. Gosh, I was trying to say something nice about him!

In any case, the swooshing of the ocean waves near my feet quickly drew my attention. The glittering blue waters were surprisingly warm to touch.

"Wow, Sirius! It's my first time seeing the ocean!"

"I suppose it is." Sirius looked like he had mixed emotions. Maybe he was dwelling on the fact that I used to be blind.

True, the forest villa was my entire world back then, but I was still young. There were plenty of places to see.

"The ocean's so weird. There's so much water coming in all the time. Is that 'cause there's lots of big fishies swimming about?"

"Those are called waves, and it's the wind that makes them sway like that."

"What? But the wind isn't blowing at all!"

"Not here, but all the way off in the distance. The waves from afar make their way over here."

"Wow...so the sea is connected to someplace far away."

Somewhere far off where I couldn't see, the wind was blowing and sending waves this way. What a mind-boggling idea. I couldn't help but stare at the incoming waves for a long, long while.

◇ ◇ ◇

After that, I was playing by the shore when Mirach made me a castle and cake out of sand.

"Wow, Mirach! It's like a real castle! Wouldn't it be great to live in?"

"Alas, Your Highness, the size would not be sufficient for your needs. Besides, you'd just get covered in sand if you tried."

"Oh, but there's cake, so I'm all set."

"You cannot eat sand. It will turn gritty in your mouth."

What could I say to that? Mirach wasn't very good at playing pretend. Not long ago, when I was reading a picture book, he even remarked, "Pumpkins cannot turn into carriages. This book is inaccurate."

Meanwhile, as I was digging my feet into the sand, Sirius came over. He picked me up and took me into the sea. This was all very fun at first, but when he waded into a deep part where even *his* feet couldn't reach the bottom, I clung to his neck in fright. Even then, he didn't stop. He held me in one arm and swam to the open sea with the other.

"S-Sirius?" I called out his name nervously, my eyes half-closed.

"Not to worry," came his cheerful reply. "I can swim you all the way over to the new continent."

"What?" My eyes stretched wide at his total lack of hesitation, which made the sheer vastness of the sea flood into my view.

As I held onto him tightly, at a loss for words, the wind started blowing gently, licking at my sides as it passed. All the while, Sirius swam toward the open sea at a brisk and steady pace. The wind tickled my face while the water stroked my body—they both felt soothing.

"Whee! I'm a fishy now!" I squealed.

Right at that moment, something jumped out of the water right next to me.

"Eeek! A big fish?!" I gawked as I clung to Sirius.

It wasn't a fish that came flying out of the ocean, though. It was Scheat.

"Ah ha ha ha! Surprised, Your Highness?"

Scheat chortled, causing Sirius to instantly yell at him.

When we left the water, I went looking for golden seashells with Canopus.

"We gotta find them for the Sea Lord," I said, scouring the shore. Sadly, I didn't spot a single one. "Hmm, if we can't find any, does that mean the Sea Lord already found them all and took them home?"

Although it was sad not to make any discoveries, it was a good thing if that meant they were in the owner's hands.

When I looked up at Canopus, he had an apologetic look on his face. "I apologize for not finding any seashells. I spent my childhood near the sea, and it was something I prided myself on."

"Oh dear, that's what you're sad about? Oh no... But, Canopus, you weren't looking for *golden* seashells back then, were you? I bet it takes a special technique to find the golden ones!"

Canopus didn't look convinced at all, but he rarely ever argued with me. "Perhaps so," he agreed, after a mopey pause.

"Yep!" I nodded. I was a kid, so if he agreed, then I believed it.

I took his hand and we went back to the villa.

In the evening, everyone gathered on the shore for dinner. As the sun sank into the horizon, the knights lit some firewood and cooked the fish they'd caught that day. It was all super yummy. I said so every time I took a bite, but the knights didn't seem so happy, even though they were the ones who prepared our entire dinner.

"Jeez, it's just fish and more fish. Why's there no red meat in the ocean?"

"I reckon it should be mandatory for the sea to have beef."

I didn't really get what they were talking about, but they ate a whole bunch like they always did. Didn't that mean they liked it? But when I asked them that, they started complaining about the size of the fish.

"They're so tiny! I got bigger catches when I came to the beach three years ago. These ones are so little, it's hard to sink your teeth into them."

"Yeah, there weren't many fish around today. I guess they went elsewhere since the water was warmer than usual."

"If I find where they're hiding, I'll round them all up!" I said blusteringly, even though I didn't manage to catch a single fish. They were all too fast for me.

The knights agreed with me, though. "That's the spirit, Princess Serafina. I bet you could catch a fish so big you wouldn't be able to hold it with both your hands!"

"Yeah, you'd get so many I wouldn't be able to fit them all in my stomach!"

They spoke with so much passion that it made me wonder if they actually thought that way...but I decided to believe them anyway. I was a kid, after all.

I cooked a breadstick over the fire after that, but I held it too close and half of it got burned. Oh well, it was my mistake, so I would have to live with it. As I munched on the charred bits, Sirius reached out and took the bread from me.

"Oh! My bread!" I tried to snatch it back with both my hands, only for Sirius to slot some beautifully baked bread between my palms. "Gosh, Sirius! Are you a baker?"

I gazed up at Sirius, startled by the soft and fluffy bread I was now holding. He looked down at me with a dashing expression. "Not a bad guess. I can be anything you need me to be, my Princess."

What a generous suggestion—I had a request straight away. "Okay, then be a knight who protects me! Then I can go anywhere, even dangerous places!"

"Ha ha ha, I always knew you were a tomboy."

But just when Sirius started to cheerfully laugh, the other knights stiffened in shock and dropped their gaze. I wondered if there was some kind of legend within the knight brigades that seeing Sirius's smile would curse you.

It was really weird to me how they refused to meet his eyes. Why were they like that when Sirius was so nice and cheerful?

◇ ◇ ◇

After dinner, everyone sat around the fire and took turns telling stories.

The tales were all very interesting, like how someone got a really good deal when they bought a horse, or that there was this cool secret technique for limiting the rust on a sword blade, or this one time someone ate the biggest hunk of meat in their entire lives.

Everyone was very engaged in the conversation...until Mirach's turn came. When he brought the tips of his fingers together and smiled, everyone looked wary. This small action tipped them off that he was about to share something really, really dull.

Eventually, Mirach launched into his tale, speaking slower than usual. None of the knights were the slightest bit interested.

"The other day, a mathematician I know told me something astounding. The ratio between a circle's diameter and circumference is an irrational number. This number has an infinite amount of decimal places!"

I didn't have the foggiest idea what he was saying.

By this point, almost every other knight had stopped paying attention, but Mirach didn't seem to notice. Eagerly, he unveiled the number he was talking about.

"3.14159265358979323846..."

Thanks to their full stomachs and the exhaustion from playing on the beach, everyone instantly started nodding off.

Scheat frantically spoke up before the damage was completely done. "Hold up! Let me have my turn before you conk out!"

I blinked my eyes open just when Scheat silenced Mirach by shoving him to the side. Everyone straightened up as Scheat cleared his throat to get the ball rolling again.

Then, as he glanced around at his audience, he began his story in a slightly hushed tone.

"This story is one of the Seven Wonders of the Crown Territory.

You may have heard other knights whisper about it. Don't quote me on whether this is true, but apparently King Regulus hid all kinds of secret treasures in this sea. They say you can find what you seek if you peer into the sea from the right location on the night of a crescent moon."

This story was so exciting compared to Mirach's that my eyes instantly flew open. "Wow! King Regulus had a secret treasure?!" I asked, my heart pounding with excitement.

King Regulus was the Spirit Lord's son and the first king of Náv. Who knew that *he* hid treasure in this sea?

Scheat nodded deeply as he went on: "He sure did! Nobody knows what it is, though. It could be money, priceless jewels, an immortality potion—you name it. But no matter how desirable the treasure is, it all belongs to King Regulus at the end of the day. So if anyone were to reach out and take it..."

He cut himself off there, then narrowed his eyes and resumed in a spooky voice.

"They'll be sucked into the sea, never to return!"

A solemn silence came over the group as Scheat finished his tale. The knights turned to look at me in worry.

I bet they were waiting for me to say something, so I clapped my hands together and cried, "Oh, I get it! So the first king *reeeeeeally* wants a friend to stay with him?"

Scheat practically fell over when I said that. "Er, uh, no, that's not what I was getting at."

"Oh? It's not?" I asked back, because I thought for sure I was right.

"I was expecting you to, uh, be more spooked," Scheat insisted as he waved his arms frantically.

"Oh, it *is* spooky! I bet he had some super valuable stuff if he had *all* kinds of treasures. It's scary to imagine losing it because of someone else."

"Uh, that's not the kind of spooky I'm talking about."

"Oh no, I'm still wrong? Ah, okay, I've got it! You know how you can't see well at night? What if you're staring into the sea for so long that you don't notice your bathing suit slip off into the ocean? Then you'd have to go home without any clothes! Oh, but that's more embarrassing than spooky, isn't it?"

"I give up." Scheat hung his head, looking awfully disappointed. His fellow knights laughed and ribbed him.

As I looked around at the knights, wondering if I'd said something bad, I noticed Seven floating a short distance away. He was peering out at the sea.

Oh, so my spirit had finally made an appearance. I wondered if he'd been sleeping this whole time—a surprising thought. I stood up and made my way over to him.

Since he'd cast an invisibility spell to hide himself from everyone except me, it looked to everyone else as if I was suddenly heading for the waves. Canopus instantly followed me in worry, so I had to explain, "You can't see him, but my spirit is there." Canopus nodded back at me with a straight face.

"Seven, were you asleep until now? Too much sleep makes it harder to nod off at night, you know?"

Seven pouted at my words. *"I didn't think I'd sleep this much. It's abnormal for me. There might be something here that lulls spirits to sleep."*

"What?"

And here I thought Seven was just being a lazy bum. I wondered if he was making up some wild story to cover up the fact that he overslept. Not that I was going to let him know what I suspected—I was a saint who cared deeply for the spirits, after all.

"Oh, you think? That must be very rough on you!"

"I know you don't believe a thing I said. Could you try a little harder to not sound like you're reading from a script?"

"Oh dear! But I put so much emotion into that!" I retorted, miffed by the criticism. I put all my effort into that act—was there really any way to improve it?

"Huh? Was that really the best you could do?" Seven muttered, before smoothly changing the subject. *"When I got here, I happened to overhear what Scheat was saying. There's something nagging me about that story, like I'm on the cusp of remembering..."*

He cut himself off there and glanced around the shore.

"There's something familiar about this place."

Seven's uncertain expression made me blink in surprise—because I'd been feeling the same way about this beach. This place was entirely made up of sand, sea, and bits of the Lodrigone continent, but for some reason it reminded me of the Forest of Lent.

"It has that nice, familiar feeling, like there are spirits living here. I wonder why." I cocked my head as I walked toward the sea.

At that moment, a large hand grabbed me from behind and hoisted me into the air. Then the hand's owner propped me on his shoulder.

"Sirius!" I called out his name as I clung to his neck for dear life.

Sirius laughed teasingly. "Is your cheeky spirit playing a trick on you? The water's dangerous, so he'd best keep his pranks above sea level."

Even though Sirius couldn't see Seven, he could tell we were talking. That was super smart of him, although he did assume wrongly that this was a prank. Neither me nor Seven intended that. "There're no tricks going on here!" we both insisted with the same breath.

Seven wasn't satisfied just leaving it at that, though, so he stuck out his tongue at Sirius. Not that Sirius could see it, since Seven had forgotten that he was invisible.

Then my spirit jumped off toward the water. As I watched him disappear into the darkness, Sirius asked, "Are you going after him?"

I looked down at Sirius and shook my head. I got the impression that Seven had gone off to see if there were any spirits around. It was better not to get in his way.

Sirius nodded and then lowered me to his chest. Normally, this would be enough to make me feel completely safe and sound, but tonight there was a restless feeling in me that wouldn't go away. What was going on here? I pressed a hand against my chest.

Sirius peered at my face, having noticed my unease. "What is it? Is something weighing on you?"

"There's something about this place that's making me all fidgety."

"That so? Might be from all that running around you did. I'm sure you're tired. Let's head back," Sirius said as he whisked me away back to the villa.

He handed me off to the ladies-in-waiting, who bathed me, changed me into my nightclothes, and put me to bed.

I knew I had to wait for Seven and ask him what the matter was...but I had no memory of what happened after that.

A Tale of the Secret Saint ZERO

Downtown Shopping

SEVEN DIDN'T WAKE ME the next day, which was very strange. When my eyes opened, I thought I must have risen earlier than usual, but the sun's position told me that it was mid-morning.

How weird of Seven to still be asleep after all that napping he did yesterday. Just as I was marveling at all the out of the ordinary things that can happen in life, Seven came bounding into the room.

"Good morning, Seven! You sure slept a ton, huh?"

"Fi, do you know what time I went to bed? It might've been super late."

"Hm? When *did* you go to sleep?"

He didn't tell me when, but knowing him, I assumed that he had to have fallen asleep early.

Instead, after a pause, he said, *"Like I told you yesterday, there's something about this place that lures spirits to sleep. By the way, I looked around the sea a little after we talked yesterday. I sensed there was a spirit around, but I couldn't find them. What's up with this place?"*

"Hmm, I have no clue. I'm going into the nearby town today; wanna search for clues with me tomorrow?"

"I might as well take a look around today by myself. I wanna check out those big rocks. It'll be quicker if I just fly there."

The beach gave me a restless feeling last night too, so I understood why Seven wanted to find out who the spirit was as quickly as he could. But sadly, I couldn't fly, so it was best for him to go alone if he was planning to check out those rocks from above.

"Okay," I answered. "If you ever feel like you wanna see the town, just drop by!"

Seven waved as he jumped out the window.

I had shopping plans today, just like I told Seven. At first, I wanted all the knights to come along, but a big group was bound to attract attention, so just six of us went: me, Sirius, Canopus, Scheat, Mirach, and Miaplacidus.

Miaplacidus was a brawny man with dark blue hair. He was formerly the top-ranked knight in the First Knight Order, which made him the second-strongest royal guard knight after Captain Deneb.

He was definitely in great shape, but unlike the other knights who thought about swords and bodybuilding all day, his mind was always on his future bride. He was kind of an odd duck.

Once, when he was guarding me, he said, *"My parents were each other's first partners when they got married, and they get along very well to this day. It's always been my dream to marry the first woman I court too. I picked this job because it has a lot of men and I don't want my wife to worry about what I'm doing after we're married."*

I was super impressed at the effort Miaplacidus put into planning, but then Scheat whispered into my ear: *"For all that talk, he still hasn't met anyone who'll date him. I mean, the knight brigades are a total sausage fest. No way he'll meet many women here. Sure, he has his big plan, but he didn't account for the fact that the ladies aren't exactly swooning over him."*

"What? But Miaplacidus looks like he's got his act together. And he's strong and kind," I answered in surprise.

Scheat had a lot to say on that topic, though. *"Exactly! He's* too *put together! He's a fun guy when you get to know him, but he sucks at breaking the ice. Whenever he meets someone for the first time, he's always got this grim look on his face. It's intimidating to most people. And since he towers over everyone, women go out of their way to avoid him."*

"What, really?!" If what Scheat said was true, then Sirius was probably in the same boat. So I asked, *"Then what about Sirius? He can be unfriendly at times, and he has a stern face too."*

Scheat's eyes boggled. *"Wh-what? Are you kidding me? You can't sum up Vice-Commander Sirius's face as 'stern.' He's what's known as a 'supreme hottie'! With looks like that, who cares about whether he's friendly or not? Anyone would try shooting their shot with him."*

I didn't get it. Sirius definitely had a nice face, but so did Miaplacidus.

"Wow, this is hard. Their looks are pretty much the same to me."

"It's like comparing a magic-enhanced mythril sword to a fake sword at a toy store," Scheat said flatly. He looked totally defeated.

I knew that Scheat was only talking about looks, but maybe he was biased because Sirius was the knight brigades' top swordsman. No way was Sirius's face a luxury item compared to Miaplacidus's.

Oh, and Miaplacidus listened to all of this without saying a word, even though he was the entire subject of the conversation. Whatever else you could say about him, he had the patience of an angel.

◇ ◇ ◇

The town was already bustling with people by the time we showed up. It was so much fun looking around at all the stores with bright decorations on display.

This area was apparently a popular tourist destination. Although we were at a private beach yesterday, the one next to it was open to everyone, plus it was the closest beach to the capital. The stores were selling a bunch of exotic trinkets, like soap bars, glittering rocks, cute seashells, and turtle shells. I spent ages just admiring everything.

Sirius's voice snapped me out of my trance. "If you stare at everything that catches your interest, we won't move ten meters by the time the sun goes down."

He teased me, but he definitely wasn't trying to make me rush.

I picked out a soap bar made out of seaweed and a sponge made out of coral, which Mirach paid for straight away and

Canopus carried. I was examining a seashell, trying to decide whether I should buy it, when Scheat pointed at something further inside the shopping district.

"You know, I came to this town three years ago as a bodyguard for one of the princes. Back then, I got a seashell accessory as a souvenir for my little sis. There's a bunch of shellcraft stores right at the end of the district."

"Oh, really? You're so smart, Scheat!" I exclaimed, since checking those out sounded fun.

"Princess Serafina, the golden seashells you heard about yesterday are simply a legend," Mirach jumped in. "This beach is even more famous for its jade shells. They're considered a local treasure. They possess a rare beauty and color, and they're often made into hair baubles, pendants, earrings, and other such things."

"Wow, that sounds lovely! I wanna see!"

Enthralled by the promise of jade seashells, I dragged everyone to the specialty craft store—only to arrive at a totally deserted street corner. It was like I'd only imagined all the hustle and bustle from before.

"Wh-what?!"

As I stared at the empty corner, Scheat let out a cry of surprise. "This is the area I was talking about! There were more than ten shellcraft stores around here three years ago. You're telling me they all closed up?!"

As Scheat mentioned, there were ten shops at the end of the busy street corner, but they all had their curtains drawn—a sign that they were closed.

The owner of the shop next door noticed us standing stock-still in shock. "Sirs, you're wasting your time!" he called out to us. "The jade shellcraft stores are gone! The last one hung on till last month, but they ran out of stock thanks to the summer rush. They closed up 'cause they don't got nothin' to sell."

"You're saying the jade shells sell so well that the stores run out of stock?" Mirach asked skeptically. "Can't they just make new wares?"

"You ain't been 'round in a while, have ya? The jade shells have gone away. The sea temperature started goin' up 'round three years ago, y'see. The shellfish are sensitive to even the tiniest change, so there's no more of 'em these days."

"What? That sounds terrible!" I blurted out, surprised by the shopkeeper's information.

"Sure is! The jade shells were our biggest local specialty! The fisherman are out of work too, since they've always sold their hauls to the craftspeople and shop owners. And that's not the only problem—with the risin' temperatures, the fish are disappearing too. Nowadays, you can only catch tiny little buggers."

"What's been making the water warmer?" asked Mirach.

The shopkeeper scowled and waved his hands. "Word has it that it's 'cause all the golden seashells are gone."

"Those weren't just a myth?" Miaplacidus spoke up. He must have been *very* surprised, since he was usually quiet when meeting people for the first time.

The shopkeeper shook his head firmly. "Nope, they're real all right. Some folks have actually spotted 'em, although there've only been a few sightings over these past few years. They're there, but they're rare. Locals say that good luck comes to anyone who sees one, so folks are always on the lookout when they go for walks, but they're not somethin' you see every day."

"I'm surprised to hear that those legendary shells actually exist. I'm sure you'd make a pretty penny if you sold them as accessories. Does no one take them off the shore?" Mirach changed the subject. He was probably wondering why he hadn't heard of any golden seashell accessories.

The shopkeeper waved his hand furiously, as if Mirach had uttered something outrageous. "That's just temptin' fate! Those shells belong to the Sea Lord. You're meant to admire them but don't never touch 'em. Nobody 'round here would dare bring them home, so you wouldn't think they'd be on the decline. Still, nobody's done spotted one in three years. The old folks are all sayin' that the Sea Lord's mad, and that's why the sea's gotten worse."

Oh right, the idea that it was bad luck to take the golden seashells away *was* part of the story I heard. Nobody would take the Sea Lord's stuff if they'd heard the legend.

"Is that so? Thank you. That was some valuable information," said Mirach. Then he bought a whole bag of colorful fruit from the man's shop. He was a very considerate person in his own way.

We walked for a while until we were a fair distance away from the shopkeeper. Then Canopus muttered, "If the golden seashells were so few in number, it must have been a challenge to sustain them. Some types of rare shellfish have disappeared entirely from my homeland, Sutherland."

Scheat was satisfied by this explanation, judging by the big nod he gave. "Makes sense! I was surprised when I heard that those legendary seashells were real, but I bet they were actually orange or something. Golden creatures don't exist, you know? Either way, the old folks believe in it, so I bet they drew a connection between their lucky item going away and the water changing."

"Yeah, I can't see how the temperatures would rise if two or three shellfish went missing," Mirach agreed. "But it's definitely a fact that the waters are warmer now. I felt it for myself yesterday, and the knights who are familiar with this area said there weren't as many fish around. Still, what caused it is anyone's guess."

"Leave the guessing to the scholars. But, darn! We're out of luck with the jade shells! What am I gonna get for my sister now?!"

Scheat was clutching his head when a gaudy-looking man approached us.

Although Scheat, Mirach, and Miaplacidus were wearing eye-catching shirts today, this fellow's outfit outdid them all. The colors were brighter, and there were a bunch of accessories dangling from his sleeves and torso. He was such a weird, novel sight that I couldn't help but look up at him in surprise.

He had a multicolored bandana on his head and dark-looking glasses on his face. It looked like he was trying to keep his face hidden, but anyone who knew him would recognize him straight away—just like I did.

What's he doing here? As I stared at him, wide-eyed, he held out a paper bag for me. "Hi, little lady! For you, okay? I bought tooooo much."

His tone was higher-pitched than normal, and his sentences sounded slightly broken. Between that and his weird outfit, I guess he was pretending to be a different person? But why was he doing that? Anyone could figure out who he was right away.

When I peered up at Sirius in hesitation, he looked unamused. If I could recognize the gaudy man, then Sirius definitely knew who he was too.

Just as I was wondering if I should leave this to Sirius to handle, the man spoke up in an even higher-pitched voice. "So heavy! So heavy! Take now, pleeeease!"

This made me reach my hand out in a panic, but Canopus cut in between us.

Seeing him on such high alert made me think: *Oh. Does he not know who this is?*

But then I saw that Scheat, Mirach, and Miaplacidus also had their hands on the swords at their hips, their expressions flashing with wariness, and it occurred to me that maybe *they* didn't know either. What a surprise!

When Canopus and the others showed their hostility, the gaudy man's bodyguards appeared seemingly out of nowhere. There were about a dozen of them. They were all in ridiculously gaudy outfits too, so you couldn't say for certain who they were, but judging by the fact that they all had their swords drawn, they were probably knights.

And indeed they were, because Canopus, Scheat, Mirach, and Miaplacidus all shouted in confusion at the newcomers. "What?!

The First Knight Brigade?! What are you doing here? And what's with the weird getups?"

"The same thing you're doing!" the First Knight Brigade members retorted. "Guard duty!"

Scheat was part of their ranks before he joined the royal guard. His former knights-in-arms must have been annoyed that he was making fun of their outfits when he was no different himself.

The banter made it clear that the twelve random swordsmen were from the First Knight Brigade. Since this unit was meant to protect the royal family, Canopus and the others figured out who the gaudy man was.

"Your M-M-Majesty?!"

"King Procyon!"

The four knights hurriedly bent their knees. Father brought a finger to his lips, looking like he was in just as much of a panic. "Shh! Shh! Don't say that name aloud! I'm just your everyday, fun-loving tourist here!"

It was already a bit late, in my opinion, since we were drawing stares from the crowd, but Father was desperate not to cause a fuss.

Before the four knights could stand up, though, Sirius stubbornly stood in Father's way. "So what exactly are you doing here?"

"What? You know meeee? I am new to this country. Who be you?"

Sirius frowned, silently staring the man down.

Father stared back at him without a peep.

But since Sirius showed no sign of backing down no matter how long they kept at it, Father took off his sunglasses with a defeated sigh and said, "Hi, I'm your uncle."

The truth was out.

Then he laughed sunnily. "Can't get one past you, Sirius! None of the knights recognized me, but you saw right through my disguise! Must be love, eh? I had no idea you were so fond of me!"

Sirius completely ignored Father's attempt at flattery, repeating: "So what exactly are you doing here?"

"Uh, well, you see, I heard the water temperature around here's been going through a bit of a strange spell, so I came to have a look! I put on a disguise since it's a top-secret mission and all. Who knew I would run into you here? What a funny coincidence!"

Sirius returned Father's cheery statement with a frigid stare. "I heard the waters started changing three years ago. You're saying that after three years, you just *happened* to go on this top-secret mission on the exact same date we're visiting? I'm pretty sure I told you well in advance that I'd be staying at the Set Villa."

"Did you now? I've been so busy these days, I can't quite remember."

"I see, then it must be a *funny coincidence* indeed that we bumped into each other. If I were the skeptical sort, I'd wonder if you chose to visit on purpose."

"Ha ha ha ha ha! Indeed! Good thing I don't have a skeptical nephew!"

Father never let anything wear him down, it seemed. He ignored the sour look on Sirius's face and turned to me, his cheeks flushed with excitement.

"Wow, Serafina! You're simply adorable! You've always looked wonderful in those frilly and lacy princess dresses, but the town girl look is cute on you too. Ah, your daddy will never forget the day he beheld his adorable, nymph-like daughter beneath the blue skies of the Set Coast!"

I had no idea how I was supposed to respond to that, so I just stared silently at my badly dressed father. But he was looking at me with shiny, expectant eyes—I knew I had to come up with something. So I blurted out the first thing that popped into my head. "I, um, won't forget the day I saw you dressed like a random wanderer either."

Father looked pleased. "A wanderer, eh? Now that's a dreamy idea. When I have some free time, I'd love to get on a camel and take you on a starry night trip to the desert."

"H-how nice. But that can't be any time soon, right? You have a lot of people depending on you. I hope your work goes well."

"Oh, Serafina, you're such a considerate daughter!" Father cast me a teary look before smiling up at Sirius. "All right, I've finished my personal business, so why don't I come along with Serafina for her shopping trip? And tonight, we can have dinner together at the villa."

Sirius was silent for a moment before painfully muttering, "I can think of no greater honor than being graced with your presence."

His contorted facial expression and tone were clearly at odds with what he was saying, but Father didn't seem to mind one bit.

As he passed me his paper bag, he said cheekily, "Here you go, Serafina. I got you the jade shell accessory you were wanting. I managed to get my hands on quite a few of these sold-out trinkets because I'm such a popular guy."

The knights stared at him wordlessly. Judging by the way they responded, I got the feeling that his shopping prowess had less to do with his popularity (real or imagined) and more to do with his kingly status. I didn't say that aloud, though, because I was a clever princess.

The bag felt heavy in my hands. There was probably enough to share with Scheat's little sister, which was a nice thought. When I glanced at him, he smiled back at me in relief...

But right then, a slender red-haired woman spoke to Scheat. "Excuse me...are you Scheat, by any chance?"

Scheat casually turned to look at the woman, but when his eyes fell on her, his body stiffened in a way that anyone could see from a mile away. He didn't say anything—he just stood there with eyes like saucers.

The woman grabbed his sleeve. "You're Scheat from Zios Village, right?" she pressed him. "I'm Lyra from Deila, the village next door! Remember me? I brought you eggs all the time. You were always scarfing them down and saying how much you liked them."

"Uh, I don't know this Scheat you speak o—"

Scheat didn't know when to give up. It was totally obvious to everyone that he knew Lyra, and the fact that she got his name right made it just as clear that she knew him. Despite all of that, he tried playing dumb.

But before he could get all the words out, Lyra interrupted him. "There's no way I could mistake you for anyone else, not with that bright yellow mop of yours. You're Shocking Blond Scheat for sure!"

The blood instantly drained from Scheat's face. Then he started trembling in a way that was *very* out of character for him. "I...no!" he shouted. "Look here, half my hair is red! I'm not blond!"

With that, he turned and ran away.

True, he had red hair on the right side of his head, but the other side *was* blond...

His actions took me such by surprise that I couldn't even move, but Miaplacidus quickly chased after him, promising, "I'll bring him back!"

Please, I thought, nodding.

Meanwhile, Lyra spoke to Mirach, who was standing close by. "Are you Scheat's friend? I'm Lyra, and I'm his friend from way back when. Could you tell him I work half the week at the candy store on this street? He can pop by when he has time."

I left Mirach to deal with her because he was good at that sort of thing. Meanwhile, Father returned with his hands full of grilled seafood. "Look, Serafina! It's fresh! Would you like squid or octopus legs?"

What a hard question.

Even though I was still worried about Scheat, I held hands with my excitable daddy, and together we went looking around a bunch of different shops.

◇ ◇ ◇

That night, Father changed back into his usual clothes, and we had dinner together. Scheat came back a short while before we ate to apologize for running away from his duty without permission. His face was tense, and I got the impression that he didn't want to talk about Lyra at all. "It's okay. I was just surprised," was all I could say.

As worried as I was about him, it was better to leave things be if he didn't want to talk. He didn't say anything to Miaplacidus either, so when Miaplacidus came back and said he didn't know the details, I told him to just keep an eye on Scheat for now.

I cheered up for dinner...although it ended up being kind of a lonely thing. The knights stubbornly insisted that they "didn't deserve a seat with His Majesty," which left only me, Father, and Sirius at the table. I thought it was a shame that our dinners were the same as they were in the castle, even after coming all the way to the Set Villa.

Father was in a good mood, though. He drank bucketloads of wine and had a lot to say. The conversation was a ton of fun, but by the time I finished my plate, I was nodding off.

Sirius noticed straight away and signaled to Canopus, who was standing in the corner. "Take Serafina to her room."

Canopus came over at once. Meanwhile, I looked at Sirius with droopy eyes and shook my head. "Nnngh… I'm still fine."

"Your cheeky spirit might be waiting for you. You'd best check in with him…if you're still awake, that is."

"Oh, right…" I said as Canopus swept me into his arms.

He carried me to my room very quietly; it was like I was being rocked by gentle waves… I was asleep long before my head even hit the pillow.

A Tale of the Secret Saint ZERO

POINT OF VIEW

SIRIUS

The First Spirit Lord

WHEN CANOPUS TOOK Serafina away, she already appeared to be half-asleep. It was the same as last night—she went to bed earlier to make up for the unusually high amount of activity she did throughout the day. She was fast asleep when I checked in on her.

Smiling, I turned back to the king. He was gritting his teeth in apparent frustration.

"Just so you know, Sirius, Serafina is *my* daughter! Not yours!"

"Well, of course," I replied, wondering why he would say something so obvious. "*I* certainly didn't give birth to her."

"Oof, that sounds worrying in another way. Anyway, I hope you're not planning on snatching her as a bride! I'll only give her over to a man who has gone through stringent testing!"

A sound plan, to be sure. But I wasn't going to let *him* be the sole judge of that.

"She's still only six, you know. And when she's older, you should be vetting the man together. Of course, she can't just make off with some ruffian no matter how much she likes him, so I'll meet him and judge his character as well. Only the men I approve of should be on your list of consideration."

"Oh? That's, well...hmm. I wouldn't want Serafina to be with a dubious fellow, but she shouldn't be single forever either. Something tells me you'd never let anyone pass your test." The king's expression scrunched in uncertainty.

Eyeing him, I decided to ask why he chose to visit. The timing was most certainly because he wanted to see Serafina, but that wasn't reason enough for a monarch to leave his station. This led me to think that he had another more pertinent task at hand.

"Is this region so important that the king must visit personally?" I asked bluntly.

I got an equally blunt answer in return. "Well, this is the royal family's biggest secret, but the first Spirit Lord lived around here."

He uttered this vital information so casually that, just for a moment, my jaw dropped, but I quickly got my wits together and cast a glance at the knights on standby in the corner of the room. Despite their efforts to blend into the background, their eyes were wide with amazement. It was clear as day that the king's voice had reached their ears.

I looked at the king, silently asking whether it was best to dismiss the knights, but he just waved his hand casually. "Let them be. Either way, I'll be needing them to stay nearby."

Okay, I see how it is. He'd cleared out everyone in the room when he told me about Serafina's blindness, but this time, he was willing to let the knights stick around. Even if he did need them around, it made me think that he regarded Serafina's secret with greater discretion than "the royal family's biggest secret." Quite a satisfying thought.

My expression must have visibly relaxed, because the king gave me a strange look. "You seem content, Sirius. Do you have a fondness for the Spirit Lord? Well, I suppose everyone is indebted to him, so he's impossible to dislike..."

He put his wine glass on the table.

"As you know, the first Spirit Lord is the progenitor of our royal family. The first child he had with a human woman became Náv's first king. And...for better or worse, much of the story of the Spirit Lord and the royal family was passed down orally. The potential risk of widespread exposure outweighed the risk of the information getting jumbled along the line."

"I see," I said plainly.

The king stroked his beard thoughtfully. "Anyway, this should go without saying, but you mustn't breathe a word of this conversation to anyone. Also, as you know...when two people of different backgrounds make a child together, the mother's lineage is what gets passed down."

This was evident in the royal family as it currently stood. I nodded, and the king went on to explain exactly that.

"Going by that rule, it stands to reason that every member of the royal family is human. Spirits have long life spans, but humans do not. When the first Spirit Lord's wife and children passed away, he said, 'I've done enough,' and hid himself away in this land."

"Did he give his title away to another spirit?" I asked. The king had mentioned multiple times that this was the "first" Spirit Lord, which made me think that the title must have switched hands.

The king nodded, proving my assumption correct. "Yes, he did. The first Spirit Lord wanted to live out the remainder of his days quietly. Normally, the title would have been passed on to a blood descendant, but since the first Spirit Lord only had human children, he gave it to the mightiest spirit at the time. His replacement...well, you might say he was the 'progenitor of the spirits.' He was around when the ancient continent of Lodrigone still existed. The longer a spirit lives, the more power they draw from the land. The second Spirit Lord was truly transcendent."

"Is he the current Spirit Lord?"

The Náv Kingdom was founded around 250 years ago. If the original Spirit Lord waited until the deaths of the first king and his siblings, then he would have passed on his title around two hundred years ago. Two hundred years was a blink of an eye compared to how long ago the Lodrigone Continent existed. Considering that, it was hard to imagine that the title had changed hands again within the past two hundred years.

King Procyon shook his head at my question. "Nobody can say. I'm sure the first Spirit Lord would have been happy to let his children know the situation, but the current Spirit Lord has no blood ties to the royal family whatsoever, so we've never even met. I don't know a thing about his circumstances."

I nodded—that made perfect sense.

The king spread his arms imploringly. "The spirits maintain the world's balance. Their power flows from the earth and then back into it. Outside influences are always altering the world...but if it's too quick or drastic, it becomes inhospitable to us humans."

It was said that spirits were manifestations of water, wind, and light. In that sense, the spirits and the earth—nature and its components—influenced each other. It was like how warm air heated up its immediate area, or how shining a light into darkness would brighten up the surroundings. If the spirits were like warm air and light, then they could influence and change the world.

That said, it was long ago when the spirits were born from nature itself. These days, they bore children through a union with a fellow spirit.

"Since the first Spirit Lord was a 'forefather spirit' from the ancient times, he drew his power from the land when it was at its youngest and healthiest. Our world maintained its balance because he returned his power to the land...but that stopped being the case two hundred years ago, when the ancient spirits pulled away from this region."

The first Spirit Lord was likely born from the ancient water, air, and light. This allowed him to wield a primordial power that no longer existed today.

"See, there are fragments of the Lodrigone Continent here. You could say it's the first Spirit Lord's homeland, a place of sentimental significance. That's why he built an invisible palace around the large rocks here. Although he has hidden himself away, fragments of his power have occasionally broken off and fallen into the sea. Thanks to that, the world's balance has been just barely maintained, but nowadays he must have holed himself up entirely, since those fragments are nowhere to be seen."

"Fragments of his power?" I asked, wondering if he was referring to some kind of metaphor.

"Yes, the objects known colloquially as the golden seashells," the king clarified. "They might look like shells, but they're actually the first Spirit Lord's tears. The tears of a powerful being naturally have power in their own right. When they dissolve in the ocean, they purify the waters. It's what was maintaining the sea temperature—that was the observable effect, at least. And surely, their influence is even more wide-reaching than that."

"Because no land is disconnected from the sea."

All right, so if I understood this correctly, the first Spirit Lord's power was felt throughout the entire world, using the sea as its conduit. And this maintained the world's balance in many different respects—for example, say, the distribution of mana.

On a personal level, I'd observed that monster populations were on the rise throughout these past three years. I now had an answer for that.

"If the shells have disappeared, it could mean that the first Spirit Lord has finally sworn off this world entirely. He built his palace in a distorted space, probably so he wouldn't interact with our world." The king sighed wearily. "He can live where he pleases, of course, and it's not my place to tell him to return his power. I know that the fate of the world shouldn't be left entirely to him alone. But I thought that, being his descendant and all, I could put in a friendly little request as family."

"A very noble idea."

Serafina's visage hovered to mind—the girl who inherited the Spirit Lord's golden eyes and could speak his language. Nobody was a more suitable messenger than her.

But...

I rapped my fingers against the table and recalled that I'd never once mentioned to the king and queen that Serafina could understand the spirit language.

Thank goodness for that. As much as he doted on his daughter, the king might have plotted to send Serafina to the first Spirit Lord if he felt the urgency for it. Alternatively, someone else might have asked her to be the messenger even if the king was opposed.

The fate of the world was too much of a burden for a six-year-old to bear.

"So you plan to meet the first Spirit Lord?" I asked, keeping my expression level as I mentally tucked away what I knew about Serafina.

"Weeeell, that was the plan, but I don't see how I can reach him. It's said that, when he left the castle, he instructed people to, 'Offer a golden seashell at the spirit palace if you ever want to reach me.' Even though I know where the palace is, the 'keys' aren't around anymore," the king said as he sank into his chair. "What am I supposed to do, bring a golden seashell to his door so that I can *get* a golden seashell? That's impossible! Quite a pickle, isn't it?"

"I see. The only way is to get one from the source." I wasn't so rude as to say it aloud, but basically we would have to do something to make the first Spirit Lord cry.

The king sighed. He was probably thinking the same thing as me. "Even if his tears flow, he's not going to meet someone he doesn't want to. I'm stuck."

As the king gazed out the window in consternation, I turned over what I knew about the first Spirit Lord in my mind.

Most of what the king told me was new, but it fit with my existing knowledge and made logical sense. The first Spirit King deeply loved his human wife, and he built the villa in Set so that he could spend time with his family back then. Perhaps his tears flowed from the loss of his wife and children. This was a place of strong memories, and now it was a reminder of the happiness beyond his reach. His tears took the form of the golden seashells, and they brought stability to the land—and even the entire planet.

"Although spirits resemble the human form, at heart they are closer to the building blocks of the world, like water and air," I said. "By forming pacts with saints, they can convert the mana in the atmosphere into magical energy. They're doing what comes naturally to them, since they're part of nature and all. But still, I never imagined that the first Spirit Lord was so powerful that he could influence the entire world."

"He's a special case. He was born during an era when the earth was in its ideal form, or so they say. That makes him a wielder of primordial power. I've heard that the spirits he keeps as retainers in his palace are of a similar vintage. They'd never go against him."

The scope of the king's story went beyond human knowledge and history. It was fortunate indeed, I thought, that the spirits didn't actively attempt to control the climate.

"Either way, the spirits wouldn't intentionally interfere with nature. They might have an effect through serving a saint or because their tears fall into the ocean, but that's as far as they'll meddle."

I chewed on that thought and then said, "All right then, so if you can't find any golden seashells, is there anything else you can use as a key to the first Spirit Lord's domain?"

I figured we'd better start with the practical issue at hand.

"Well, about that..." The king rested his chin on his hands in an undignified way. "See, there's a forest that's an hour's horse ride away from here. I heard there were some trees around with golden fruit. Someone told me that you could offer it to the spirit palace in place of a golden seashell...but I was just a child when I heard that. I can't tell you whether that was part of the oral tradition or just an old wives' tale."

Watching the king as he chuckled, I gained a new appreciation for the fickleness of oral history. But still, despite the vagueness of his memories, we had nothing else to go on. We had to scope the place out.

"All right," I said after some consideration. "We'll look for both. Tomorrow, we split up into two groups: One will search for the golden seashells, and the other will search for the fruit."

"Good idea, Sirius. I can always count on you. But you'd best take your time adapting to the forest. The spirits influence every inch of the world. Being the closest forest to the Spirit Lord's domain, I'm sure that the monsters there are more active there than anywhere else."

"I'll keep an eye out," I replied, glancing toward the wall. The knights looked deflated.

"Darn it, no more vacationing on the job!"

"Yeah! I knew it was too good to be true! Oh well, at least the beach and the shopping trip were nice!"

They'd just been privy to the secrets of the first Spirit Lord, but it seemed that their main takeaway was the loss of their vacation time. I felt like I'd caught a glimpse at their ethos.

"They're full of the human spirit, at least," I muttered.

The Hidden Palace and the Crybaby Spirit

THE NEXT MORNING—well, day—I woke up when the sun was high in the sky. The last thing I remembered was Canopus carrying me to my room.

Seven must have overslept too because nobody came to wake me up. I guess this place really did have that kind of effect on him too. *Yay for resorts!* I thought as I sprang out of bed.

After the ladies-in-waiting helped me get changed, I stepped out of the room and found Canopus waiting for me in the hallway.

"Canopus! Thanks for carrying me to my room yesterday. I went to bed without brushing my teeth, so I brushed three times this morning!" I said, trying to show off what a good princess I was.

Canopus blinked in confusion. "That is...good to hear."

"Tee hee hee!"

Canopus escorted me to the dining room, where Sirius was reading through a document. "So you're awake now, Sleeping Beauty? I was starting to get worried that you'd sleep for years."

"Nuh-uh! I'll wake up straight away if you nudge me."

"But then you'd hurl a pillow at the offender. That should be my last resort."

As I sat down and chowed down on my meal, I glanced around and realized that things were quieter than usual.

"Oh? The knights aren't around. Are they sleeping in? Maybe I'm the early bird!"

"Good guess, but no. They got up when the sun rose. Half of them went to the sea, and the other half went to the forest."

"Whaaaat?! Why so early? And they're already playing without me? Why'd they leave me out?!"

"Finish your plate first."

As I obediently took a mouthful, my eyes wandered over to Sirius. "Scheat wasn't himself yesterday. Do you think it's right of me to leave him until he's ready to say what happened?"

Sirius gave me a small smile. "No other princess cares about her individual knights like you do. Scheat's an adult, so he can handle himself. I'm sure even a guy like him has a thing or two in his past that he doesn't want to bring up. Sometimes, the kind thing to do is leave it alone."

There was something in his tone that made me squint at him, but his answer made it sound as if he didn't know anything.

Except he *did* know something.

That's what my gut was telling me, but I could tell from his expression that he wasn't going to tell me. "Okay," was all I could say. He probably had a good reason for telling me to leave Scheat alone. That thought made me feel better.

As I went back to my food, marveling on how easily Sirius could put me at ease, Seven came up and sat in the seat next to me.

"It's been a while since I last saw your cheeky spirit," Sirius remarked, which made me realize that Seven wasn't hiding himself.

I looked at him, wondering if he'd had a change of heart, only to find him with his head plonked on the table, pouting rather rudely.

"Something about this place drains my energy. I guess I'm relaxed? I don't care if everyone can see me."

This was a total one-eighty from his previous attitude, so I had to wonder what was going on. Maybe this place had a soothing effect on spirits? He used to be an early riser, but now he was sleeping in too. That was a good change from my perspective, so I wasn't going to complain.

"Seven, you said you were going to have a look around yesterday. Did you find anything?"

"Hmm, it's hard to say. There's definitely something around that cluster of big rocks, but whatever it is has a powerful invisibility spell around it. I thought my power was pretty strong, but I guess I'm nothing special if I found nothing after a whole day of looking."

Seven was unusually depressed.

"Oh dear! Well, um, would you like to go out searching with me today? You might spot something you couldn't see yesterday."

"I know where the 'something' is. It's on top of the big rocks. You can't get up there, and I wouldn't recommend you try."

"Oh..."

As I copied Seven and flopped my head on the table, I realized that Father wasn't around either.

"Sirius, where did Father go?"

"Someone came by early in the morning and said there was urgent business back at the castle. He really wanted to say good-bye to you before he went, but his attendants insisted there was no time, and they all shoved him into the carriage. The coachman drove off before the king could protest, so now he's on his way back to the capital."

"Oh no! Did something bad happen?"

"He left his schedule hanging to come here, and now he's paying for it. That's all. The queen and the other nobles were in charge while he was away, and she insisted that he come back to do his job. She was pretty livid, I hear."

"Oh dear..."

Mother was put in a tough spot, so I couldn't blame her. *Good luck, Father.*

In the end, I decided to go with Seven to the rock cluster after brunch. Sirius went out to supervise the knights, so it was Canopus who came along as my guard.

It must have been Canopus's first time seeing Seven, because his eyes went wide in shock and he didn't say a word. He smoothed over his expression quickly, though. I thought it was super cool how he could do that. Someone like me or Scheat could never!

I really wanted to copy his cool and collected attitude, so I went for three minutes without saying anything, but then my mouth felt all funny and restless. I guess the cool style was not for me, not yet at least. But I was still only six, so maybe I'd get there by the time I was his age.

Yep, that's what I told myself.

Anyway, when we were directly below the cluster of rocks, I was astonished by how huge they were. "Whoa! They're like mountains!"

Each rock was about ten meters tall and five meters long, so when you put them all in a row, they looked super imposing. No matter how carefully I looked, there were barely any footholds, so climbing had to be the last resort.

I decided to split the task with Seven. "Seven, could you look above the rocks while I look below?"

Seven could fly and check the top area, while I could walk along the sands and scour the bottom.

The rocks were smack bang in the middle of the crescent-shaped beach, but there was enough space for a person to walk through them from either end. It was possible to get from one end of the beach to the other.

"Makes sense. Okay, we'll check each rock out at the same time. I'll take the top and you take the bottom."

At first, I looked up at each rock to check Seven's position before looking down at the part I was meant to look at, but then I figured out that I could tell where he was from his reflection in the water.

"Hmm, I wonder why I can see Seven's reflection in the water from this angle when he's all the way above the rocks?"

Maybe Seven was right and there was a mysterious power at work in this area. But it sure was convenient, I thought.

Just as I was checking the nineteenth rock, I noticed that Seven's reflection had disappeared.

"Hey, Seven, where did you go?" I asked worriedly.

"What do you mean? I'm on top of the rock," Seven's voice replied evenly. *"Look, I'm standing by the edge. You should be able to see from where you are."*

"No, I can't see you."

"Say what?!"

After a short while, Seven appeared past the three rocks ahead of me. "Oh, I can see you now! Where did you go?"

"I was just flying over the rocks like normal... Seems like you couldn't see me only when I was going over those three rocks."

"What? How can this be?!" I exclaimed.

Then I remembered what Scheat was saying about "the Seven Wonders of the Crown Territory."

"This story is one of the Seven Wonders of the Crown Territory. You may have heard other knights whisper about it. Don't quote me on whether this is true, but apparently King Regulus hid all kinds of secret treasures in this sea. They say you can find what you seek if you peer into the sea from the right location on the night of a crescent moon."

Then there was the local legend about the sea.

"This area is known as 'the golden sea' because of the glimmering golden shells that occasionally wash ashore. People say that the shells

belong to the Sea Lord, so it is bad luck to take them away from the shore."

What's more, Sirius said before that not all legends or rumors were passed down accurately. It was daytime right now, and the moon wasn't out. Maybe "the night of a crescent moon" was actually "the crescent-shaped beach." And maybe "all kinds of secret treasures" were hidden right here...

"I've got it, Seven! You gotta put the 'Seven Wonders of the Crown Territory' and the legend of the golden seashells together! What if the Sea Lord's treasure is hidden above those three rocks where I couldn't see you? Maybe it's even got something to do with the spirits! That's why you were able to sense something."

"Sounds interesting, but you're just making a guess based on myths and legends. Still, there's definitely something hidden above this rock. If it's a treasure trove like you say it is, then it's got to be big enough to spread out across these three massive rocks."

Talking to Seven was getting me excited. I really, *really* wanted to see what the Sea Lord's treasure was.

"I'll climb up too, Seven! Let's both look for the treasure!"

But as soon as those words left my mouth, Canopus hurriedly closed in on me. As my protector, of course he didn't want me climbing any rocks, but when I insisted that I wanted to climb up them anyway, he hesitated for a moment before saying, "Please excuse me."

He picked me up and perched me on his right shoulder.

"My apologies, but I'll need to use both my hands. Please use your own arms to cling to me."

"Okay!" I chirped back.

I had no idea what Canopus was planning, but I did what he said and clung to his head. He took off the cloth around his waist and wrapped it around me instead, tying me to his body. Then he approached a rock and put his hands on the indents (on the eighteenth rock, by the way, not the nineteenth rock where Seven and I suspected the *something* was). It was the small details like this that showed how cautious he was about even the mere possibility of danger.

Then he hoisted his torso up and stuck his feet in the indents, using both his hands and legs to climb swiftly up the rock.

"Oh! W-wow!" My eyes widened.

Canopus finished climbing while I was still getting over my shock. He was so fast it left me reeling.

"You're, like, the amazingest! You can carry me *and* climb rocks!" I pumped my fist at Canopus to show my excitement, but he just shrugged as if it wasn't a big deal. "Oooh, that's what makes you so awesome! Next time I do something cool, I'll shrug and say nothing too."

After that declaration left my lips, I stood on the middle of the rock and looked around.

"Oh, there's nothing here. Just a few plants."

Though there were some grass and trees growing on the rock, most of it was empty space. But since all the rocks around here were connected, I could walk to the one that *really* had my attention next door.

The ground was so far below me, though, that just walking made me very nervous. Following Seven, who was floating in the air, I took one careful step at a time.

But then, all of a sudden, something crashed into my head.

"Whaaaa—?!"

It hit me quite hard, enough to send me flying backward and land on my bum.

"Princess Serafina?!" Canopus rushed over and helped me sit up.

But I couldn't even make a sound because my head hurt so much. After a bit of writhing in pain, I finally let out a bloodcurdling scream.

"Oooooooouch!"

I saw nothing in my way, so whatever it was, I bumped into it full-on.

As I looked up, clutching my head, my eyes met with Seven, who looked like he had just seen a ghost. *"What did you bang into, Fi?"*

His surprise only made sense because there was nothing but empty space in front of me.

"Er, um, I dunno. What *did* I hit my head on?"

How weird. It was definitely something hard. I reached a hand out—and yep, there was something.

"Whaaat?"

I sprang up and patted down the invisible object. Through some weird trick or whatever, the bit I touched appeared in front of me, revealing itself as part of a wall. Or maybe it was better to say that it *turned* visible.

"No way!"

The visible bit expanded from where I touched it. Within the blink of an eye, a pearly white palace showed up across the three massive rocks.

It was such a surreal sight that I couldn't help but stare slack-jawed at it. But no matter how many times I blinked, the palace didn't disappear. The grand, majestic building stood there right in front of me, reaching up into the sky.

When I took a closer look, there were a bunch of trees around that were just as tall as that stately-looking palace, which I found odd. I got the impression that there must be more trees inside the palace. A shallow pool of water at my feet glimmered in the sun, and I noticed that there were also some fountains lining the outside.

I was speechless at this strange, nonsensical, unheard-of sight. As the silence fell over us, I heard some small, scraping footsteps.

I looked up with a start. *Is that the owner?* I wondered.

There was a boy peering at us from the shadow of a tree.

◇ ◇ ◇

The boy, who looked about ten or so, had a startlingly beautiful face. Judging by his long, bottle-green hair—which fell all the way down to his feet—and his pointy ears, he was not human but a spirit.

The boy slowly walked up to me in a wide-eyed stupor and stared.

What was *he* so shocked about? "Um? Excuse me..." I tried to ask a question, but he just reached a hand out toward me as if he didn't hear what I was saying at all.

Suddenly, his hand stopped in the air without touching me.

Looking closely, I could see his hand was trembling. Moving my gaze from his hand, I noticed that at some point his entire body had started shaking. His face was pale, like he'd just seen a ghost.

"Er, um, is something wrong...?" I said worriedly, but he just mumbled something quietly.

I waited patiently until he spoke up again in a shaky voice.

"Lu...Luntia."

It was a name I'd never heard before, but I got the impression that he thought it was my name. Thinking that I'd better correct him quickly, I said nervously, "Um...my name is Serafina."

The boy looked like he didn't understand me, so I switched to the spirit language. *"Nice to meet you. I'm Serafina."*

The boy's reaction was immediate. He stiffened visibly, and big tears started sliding down his face.

"Huh? Wh-what's wrong? Are you hurt?" I rushed to ask, but the boy didn't answer. He didn't even budge from where he stood. The tears just kept falling.

I forced myself to wait, and eventually the boy reached his hand out again. This time, he took my hand.

"I...knew you weren't her. But you're the spitting image of Luntia! You look like her in every single way, but you have my eyes. And you can speak the spirit language, even though you're human. It's a miracle..."

He kept his grip on my hand as loud sobs erupted from his mouth.

Right then, inexplicably, rain started to pour violently around us.

"What? Rain?" Canopus hurriedly stripped his shirt and held it over me so that I wouldn't get wet, but it was a flimsy defense. I was drenched in seconds.

We couldn't just leave the wailing spirit alone while we took shelter, so the rain pelted us as we waited for the boy to calm down. By the time he noticed the downpour, we looked like drowned rats. The sight seemed to quiet him down, and he stared at our drenched bodies in blank amazement.

"Huh? You humans are so frail and weak. Why are you standing out in the rain?"

Hmm. It probably wasn't a good idea to say, "Because we didn't want to leave a kid alone." So instead I simply said we liked the rain.

It was probably a coincidence, but the rain stopped at the exact moment the boy was done crying.

He frowned in confusion at my answer before turning around and pointing at the palace. *"Come with me. I'll get you a change of clothes."*

But when Seven and I tried to follow him, Canopus cried, "Wait! I don't understand what this palace is. Although I've never heard of a spirit harming a human, you never know what can happen! I'm the only one guarding you today, and there is only so much I can do. I suggest we return to the Set Villa for now."

Canopus made a good point, so for a moment I stood there in indecision.

The boy spoke up. Although he didn't understand what exactly Canopus said, the vibe had clearly gotten across. *"Your guard seems to be wary. I want you to know that I would never do anything to hurt you, Serafina. I swear it upon my honor as a spirit. Oh, and...I haven't told you my name yet, have I? I'm Oligor."*

Seven recoiled the moment the spirit introduced himself. I guess he was taken aback that Oligor said his name so easily, because spirits only revealed it as a sign of trust. I, too, was surprised by how open he was. The Forest of Lent had plenty of spirits who were even younger than he was, and they were way more cautious.

I turned back to Canopus and gave him a firm nod to reassure him. "Canopus, this spirit told me his name. It's the highest proof of trust from a spirit, and it means he'll never betray me. So don't worry, he's not going to hurt us."

Canopus answered with a question. "Can you understand the spirit language, Princess Serafina?"

"Yep, since I've always been around the spirits."

Canopus said nothing for a moment, though I heard an audible gulp. "Your powers extend that far?" he muttered tremblingly.

"Huh? Did you say something?"

"I am berating myself for failing to grasp my liege's worth."

I couldn't help but blink at Canopus's show of sincere remorse. It wasn't every day you met someone who had lived among the spirits, and Canopus was only now finding out about this part of my life. Uh oh, maybe he was gonna decide that I had too much freedom and that I wasn't good enough as a princess. Maybe the reason he was so pale was because he regretted being my personal knight.

"D-don't you worry, Canopus! I'm still gonna be a good princess!"

"I am well aware. I vow to spare no effort and will serve you to my fullest."

"Er, um, okay? That sounds good? So, uh, we can all go in, right? We might not get another invitation if we turn back now."

Canopus nodded, so I turned back to Oligor. *"Thank you, Oligor. We—"*

But I couldn't finish my sentence because, for some reason, Oligor was crying again.

"I...can't believe it. I never thought the day would come when someone looking so much like her *would say my name so perfectly!"* He sniffled.

"Huh? You'll cry just from someone saying your name? But you're bigger than Seven... Is there something making you cry?" I asked, puzzled.

"Luntia always called me 'Ligon,'" Oligor answered tearfully.

It seemed like Oligor's friend, the one who looked like me, couldn't say his name correctly. Her pronunciation was pretty good, though, as far as things went. The spirit language was very high-pitched, so most people weren't able to pick up all the sounds. Oligor must have wanted his beloved friend to say his name the right way. I guess it made him happy to hear it from someone who resembled her.

Oligor was still weeping, but he used one hand to wipe his tears and the other to guide me into the palace.

That's how I ended up in the spirit palace for the first time—and it really was a mysterious place. Just like I imagined, some of the big trees were inside the walls too. There was even a big circle of flowers blooming beyond the tree branches, which I hadn't been able to see from the outside. Colorful butterflies perched on the flowers, and the bright sunlight coming in through the many windows made all the scenery look like something out of a picture book.

The sheer beauty left me in awe, but Oligor seemed used to it. He ushered me through without much fuss and showed me into a big, wide room. There was so much light streaming in from all directions that it felt like I was outside. Not only was there plenty of space, there were a bunch of sofas and tables around too.

"Sit wherever you like," Oligor told me, but since I was sopping wet, I didn't want to get on one of the sofas.

As I stood there feeling awkward, Oligor snapped his fingers, summoning giant cloaks to appear over all our heads. The cloak draped my body, did a quick spin around me, and disappeared.

"Huh?"

Weirdly enough, my arms, legs, and hair were instantly dry. I was also wearing different clothes from before.

"Wh-whoa, Oligor! How'd you do this?"

"Just a bit of spirit hospitality. Consider the clothing a gift."

The spirits raised special plants, which they fed to special insects, which then created a special thread to make special clothes. Seven's clothes were the same in that way. It was unheard of for spirits to share their clothes with anyone who wasn't a spirit—they were *that* special. But then again, I was only six, and there were a lot of things I didn't know.

I was a little worried about Seven, who looked a bit pale but was floating next to me speechless for once. But he said, *"I'm fine,"* which told me that he wanted to be left alone, so I turned my attention back to Oligor.

"Take a seat, Serafina," he insisted, so I plopped down on the nearest sofa.

Seven wordlessly sat down next to me, and Canopus stood behind me.

◇ ◇ ◇

Oligor sat on the sofa across from me. He peered at my face intently from across the table that separated us.

I was happy to let him stare. I bet he was thinking about his friend.

Oligor seemed to be as weepy as ever, because sure enough, his eyes started welling with tears again as he gazed at me. I used this chance to stare back at him and realized that he seemed to be crying more out of happiness than sadness.

"Oligor, why are you happy-crying?" I tilted my head.

"Because I am *happy. Serafina, your existence is a miracle to me. I never had any children who looked like Luntia. But not only do you look exactly like her, you have my eyes too. I've always pined for a link between the two of us, and now you're here."*

I tilted my head further, confused about what he was saying. *"But aren't you, like, ten? Why are you talking about having kids when you're a kid yourself? Although I do have golden eyes like you, yeah."*

"Yes...the exact same."

With a tearful smile, Oligor reached across the table and clutched my hand tightly. I could see he was happy because I looked like his friend while having his eyes—it was like the best of both worlds, I guess?

"Serafina, are you happy? Nothing is troubling you? I'd do anything for you. But...I don't have much strength left. I was planning to let my body fade away and flow back into the world."

I was stunned at that last bit. Moments ago, he casually told me his name, and now he was saying he'd help me out with just as much ease. That was very nice of him and all, but why was he talking about not having much strength left when he was still just a kid?

"What? Your body is weak? Remind me to get you a get-well-soon present next time I visit! Is there anything you like eating?"

"Let's see... I've always been partial to that sweet red fruit Luntia gave me once a long time ago."

"Okay, so you want a sweet red fruit! I'll bring you some next time." Then a sudden thought occurred to me. *"Is this your house, Oligor? Why'd you build it here? Does this Luntia person come by to visit?"*

Oligor smiled merrily. *"Ha ha, you're so full of questions. You're just as talkative as her...although I never really understood what she was saying. She was a human girl, but she couldn't speak the spirit language like you can."*

Then his gaze fell.

"Luntia doesn't come by anymore," he said sadly. *"I've come to terms with that, but there are times when I remember her, and I get lonely. I built the palace in this area because I have plenty of happy memories with her here."*

"You must be a really strong spirit to build such a marvelous place," I said. If he was weak now, the palace was proof that he must have been super strong in the past.

Just then, Seven gave me a startled look. "What's the matter?" I asked.

"Well, of course he was strong! Fi, you've gotta mind your mann—"

"Seven, was it?" Oligor cut in gently. *"Serafina is right. I'm a ten-year-old child, I'm fond of a human girl named Luntia, and now my strength is a shadow of its former self. Nothing more, nothing less."*

For some reason, Seven sprang straight up at those words. *"Yes, of course!"* he said with unusual briskness. *"I would never dare claim otherwise!"*

I raised an eyebrow at Seven's weirdly obedient attitude, but then Oligor twirled and pointed around himself. *"There are a few other spirits living here, Serafina. Unlike me, they're all adults, and they can do many things that I cannot. It was actually them who built the palace, and they take care of the garden too."*

"Oh, that makes sense." I nodded, satisfied. I was wondering how a weak child like Oligor built this palace, but now that I thought about it, it was ridiculous to think that only one spirit lived here or that he built the place by himself.

The Forest of Lent was the same. The adult spirits put the forest in place and cast an invisibility barrier around it so that the children could live there in peace.

"Oh yeah, I couldn't see this palace at first, but when I touched it, I could. Well, more like I banged my head on an invisible wall, and that's when I noticed there was something." It was kind of an afterthought, but I belatedly explained how I came across the palace.

Oligor's eyebrows knitted into a frown. *"Ah, I'm sorry about that. I put a bit of a spell on the palace. Besides the current residents, it only appears for people who share my blood."*

"Share your blood?" I blinked. *"Oh, right! I do have some spirit blood in me! My ancestors from super long ago were spirits. I guess that explains why I could see your palace."*

Right, the first king of Náv was born from a human woman and the Spirit Lord. But that was so many generations ago, and

I looked nothing like a spirit, so I was pleasantly surprised that Oligor had noticed.

When I gave him an impressed look, he cracked a small smile. *"That's not quite what I meant...but ah, Serafina, you're so pure. That's not like me at all, so you must have gotten it from Luntia. I'm amazed that a part of her could persist so far down the bloodline... She lives on in you."*

As Oligor said this, he started tearing up again. He really was kind of a crybaby, I thought. When I reached out and patted him on the head, he stiffened for a moment and then said, *"Keep going."*

So not only was he a crybaby, he was a kid who was starved for attention.

I chatted with Oligor about all kinds of things after that, but Seven barely contributed to the conversation at all. He just said things like "Uh-huh" and "interesting" instead of anything original. He was only ever around spirits he already knew in the Forest of Lent, so I guess he was the type to be shy around strangers, huh?

After a nice long chat, we decided to leave the palace for now. Talking with Oligor made me realize that this palace was not "the Sea Lord's treasure trove" like I assumed it was. As Oligor explained it to me, it was a refuge for a small population of spirits who wanted an easygoing life.

"Some parts of that legend you told me were on point," Oligor said, but he was obviously just trying to make me feel better. The reality was totally different from the stories.

When we were leaving the palace, I asked Oligor about our new clothes. Was it really okay to take them with us? But he waved my question off with a smile and told me not to worry about it.

"Those clothes have the spirits' blessing on them. They're bound to bring you good luck."

"Thank you, but, well...I do feel bad about getting a whole new outfit. The ones we were wearing just got a bit wet. I'm sure they were fine."

"Fi, these clothes are tailored to our sizes. Nobody else could wear them! Just smile and accept them." Seven, who had barely said a word throughout all of this, suddenly insisted in a panic.

I guess he really wanted the clothes. To be fair, they did look good on him.

"Thank you! I appreciate it! I'm happy to have them because they're so cute!" I said with a smile, which made Oligor blush with happiness.

After that, we waved each other goodbye.

"See you later, Serafina. I hope you come by again!"

"Yep! I'll bring some sweet red fruit next time!"

With that promise to my newfound friend, I left the spirit palace.

A Tale of the
Secret
Saint
ZERO

Vlad Forest

THREE DAYS WENT BY after my visit to the spirit palace, and sadly, it rained the whole time. Apparently, rain was rare in this region—the knights gazed out the window and said, "The spirits are weeping."

This was a saying people used whenever it rained at an unexpected time, but it made me think of Oligor's crying. By pure coincidence, it rained exactly when he cried. Anyone who saw that would be tempted to think that there was a link between rain and a spirit's tears. As I looked at the pouring rain, I thought: *No wonder that expression exists.*

What I had wanted to do was go to Vlad Forest, which wasn't very far from the villa. I was pretty sure that I could get red fruit for Oligor there. But Sirius stopped me; he was more overprotective than I thought.

He told me that I'd catch a cold if I went to the forest while it was raining, so then I suggested going to the beach because I'd get wet there anyway, but he turned that idea down as well.

Well, phooey. I couldn't go *anywhere*. As much as I grumbled, I didn't want to worry Sirius, so I spent the next three days reading some picture books that I'd brought from the capital.

Seven often popped in and out of the villa, not really affected by the weather, and sometimes he stuck around with me. I tried talking to him about Oligor, but he wasn't very chatty.

"You should make friends with Oligor," I suggested. "I bet you don't see many spirit children outside the Forest of Lent."

He pulled a reluctant face. *"He...might look like a kid, but friends? No way, he's too far above me. I could never."*

"What, is Oligor scary?"

Seven fell silent midway through the conversation, which was very weird for him.

I decided to change the topic because I didn't want to push it if it made him so uncomfortable. "You don't have to force yourself to be his friend if you don't want to. Anyway, there's a bigger problem..."

The only other person in the room was Canopus. I kept my picture book open as I muttered, quietly enough so that he wouldn't hear...

"It's Scheat."

Yep. For the past three days, Scheat had been going to Vlad Forest (the place Sirius said I wasn't allowed to go), and he'd come back with major injuries every time.

As it turned out, the knights weren't going to the forest or sea to play like I had assumed—they told me that they had a mission to do. But they were just doing a search, so why would anyone get injured? Not to mention that Mirach and Miaplacidus went to the forest too, and they only got tiny scrapes. Why was Scheat the only one getting hurt?

I was shocked the first time I saw his wounds and rushed to heal him, but Sirius stopped me. "Leave him, Serafina."

"What? B-but—!"

"When someone in the Knight Brigade gets carried away and hurts himself, our rule is to heal the bare minimum and leave them alone for half the day. Otherwise, the hotheads in our ranks are bound to repeat the same mistakes. This is for Scheat's own good. He's got to experience the pain of his injuries for himself so that he doesn't get reckless next time."

But Scheat didn't learn his lesson like Sirius said he would. He came back with big wounds the next day, and the day after that.

When I asked Mirach how Scheat got hurt, Mirach clenched his jaw. "I don't know. What I do know is that Scheat's making a bigger ass of himself than usual. He seems convinced that he's got to kill every last monster in Vlad Forest. He just goes after them by himself, without listening to anyone."

Later that day, when Sirius came back from his rounds, I was pacing around the room, my thoughts full of Scheat. Sirius raised an eyebrow at me in exasperation, but he still offered up a little bit of information.

"Serafina, you don't have to worry so much. Scheat doesn't want people to know this, but he was actually born around here.

I'm sure he's dealing with his feelings about coming back to his homeland after so much time away."

I looked at Sirius in surprise. How did he know something that Scheat was trying to hide? In response, he put a finger to his lips, letting me know that this was all a secret.

"The First Knight Brigade exists to guard the royal family," he said. "Everyone assigned there goes through a background check just in case."

I nodded because that made sense, but that didn't stop me from worrying about Scheat or from pacing around my room. So I made a decision. As much as Sirius was worried about me catching a cold, I was going to follow Scheat into the forest tomorrow, rain or shine.

But right then, there was a commotion around the villa's entrance.

I ran over, wondering what the fuss was about...and there was a knight lying there covered in blood.

I could tell who he was at a glance. His red and blond hair was a dead giveaway.

"Scheat!"

Though he'd been hurt yesterday and the day before that, he'd always managed to walk by himself. This time, though, he had collapsed, unconscious, on the ground.

Oh no! I raced up to him, only to discover another shocking fact: All the other knights around him were hurt too. They were seasoned veterans who'd barely suffered any scratches thus far, but now their uniforms were all ripped up, and blood poured from their wounds.

As much as I freaked out and wondered what had happened, I also knew what I had to do. I was about to heal Scheat, who had the worst injuries, but right then…

"Please let me heal Scheat! My magic is depleted right now, but I know I can heal him if I take a magic restoration potion!"

A frantic cry rang out across the foyer.

I looked at the owner of the voice in surprise. Scheat's childhood friend, whom we'd bumped into in town the other day, was looking at us with desperate eyes.

A Tale of the Secret Saint ZERO

POINT OF VIEW
SCHEAT

A Survivor's Parting Gift

When I was born, my hair was just one color.

People had a nickname for me because of my bright yellow hair: Shocking Blond. Like the color black, yellow was often a warning sign in nature. My hair was a bad omen to my family and neighbors. It told them that I was not someone to get close to, someone too foolish for their own good.

But I was ignorant. The day I turned ten, I walked into a forest crawling with monsters—and that same night, they attacked my village.

In mere hours, I lost my father, my mother, and my older brother and sister. So many other villagers were killed too.

Half my hair turned red after that, as if to remind me that it was my stupidity that cost everyone their lives.

◇ ◇ ◇

"Come back, Scheat! Don't give chase by yourself!"

I could hear my fellow knights shouting. But although their voices rang in my ears, I didn't pay them any heed.

I *had* to take down as many monsters as I could. Every last monster in this world had to die. I would bathe in their blood, and when every inch of my hair turned red, my sin would finally be atoned...

"Scheat!"

I was still chasing after a monster, my mind in a haze, when all of a sudden someone grabbed my arm. I didn't have to turn around to know who it was—the voice belonged to Miaplacidus.

I tried to yank my arm free, but when I couldn't pull it out of his stubborn grip, he swung around and threw me a glare. "Let go of me! The monster's getting away!"

But Miaplacidus's calm expression didn't flicker. "You've hunted enough monsters for now," he said levelly. "It's time to call it a day."

"But I—!"

"You need to conserve your strength. We have tomorrow and the day after that."

My head suddenly cleared. He was exactly right. As the tension left my body, I returned my sword to its sheath.

If my friends hadn't been there to stop me, I would have gotten myself killed a long time ago. I knew that...

I was born twenty-two years ago in Zios Village, an hour's horse ride away from the Set Coast. I had the best childhood you could ask for, surrounded by a large family and the lush countryside.

But that all changed when I turned ten.

"The spirits bless you on your birthday. It's your day of good fortune."

My parents and the adults in the neighborhood were always saying that. It was just a way of saying happy birthday, but my dumb ass took it literally. I went into a monster-inhabited forest to pick herbs for my dad since he was saying that he had a sore back from work. Plenty of herbs grew near the entrance of Vlad Forest, which would have been enough for me normally, but I was convinced that I wouldn't come across any monsters on my birthday.

So I ventured deeper than usual and plucked some high-quality herbs. Then I went home, feeling really proud of myself. I didn't even notice that the monsters had spotted me and followed me back.

It was only after the fact, when a horde of them attacked the village, that I realized what had happened. When my father, mother, older brother, and older sister died. The village was in a blaze, and most of the residents had perished. They'd all been so nice to me, and...

I don't remember what happened for a while after that.

I must have done *something* because even though I don't recall having slept or anything for months after, everything from that time was a haze. None of it remains with me. I guess I must have been in a dreamlike stupor the whole time, just going through the motions.

I came back to my senses about half a year after my tenth birthday. I realized that I was living in an unfamiliar house, surrounded by unfamiliar people. I was with the survivors of Zios Village, and we were living as family in a strange, distant town.

From afar, we looked like an elderly couple and their two grandkids.

My newfound family—the four of us were all that remained of Zios Village.

The tragedy was what brought us together, and that family gave me a new life. When Grandma and Grandpa passed away, it was up to me to raise my sister, who was two years my junior, by myself.

I was confident in my physical strength, if nothing else, so I worked literally from dawn to dusk. But that still wasn't enough to make ends meet, so when I turned fourteen, I threw everything into becoming a knight. I left my sister in the care of a friendly neighborhood landlady and sent her my entire salary...although after a while, the landlady insisted that it was too much and I slowly cut down the amount I sent.

My first deployment was the Sixth Knight Brigade, whose main job was slaying monsters. When I got the notice, I felt like I'd landed my dream job, that it was fate's hand at work.

My hair was blond at birth, and the right half got soaked in blood the day my family and friends were killed. Ever since then, that half of my hair stayed red no matter how much I washed or cut it. Maybe that was a sign from the heavens, the color of my sin. *Your foolishness got your family and village killed, and you should never forget it.* Or maybe it signified my family's regret, because it was *their* blood that got absorbed in my hair.

Either way, my red hair had a meaning, and I was convinced that if the last bit of blond in me soaked up monster blood, I would finally be free of my crimes.

So I *had* to kill the monsters. Exterminate every last one of them from the face of the earth. When this was done, their blood would turn my hair completely red—of this, I was certain.

But my dream never came true. I fought too recklessly.

The higher-ups decided that monster slaying wasn't for me, and they reassigned me to the First Knight Brigade.

◇◇◇

My first job after I joined the ranks was to accompany one of the princes to the Set Villa as his guard. It was my first time being so close to my hometown since the incident, and the nervousness made me physically ill. My knights-in-arms were worried about me, but I couldn't bring myself to tell them about my past. I was determined to take my origins to my grave.

I knew I was running away, but I didn't have it in me to confront my trauma. If I had to admit it, some part of me also knew that I was wrong about how killing monsters would lessen my sin. Even if every last monster in the world were to disappear, it wouldn't bring back my father, mother, brother, sister, or any of the villagers who had been kind to me.

It didn't matter what I did. My day of redemption would never come. I would never be able to escape my sin. One day, it would catch up to me, and every last blemish on my soul would be exposed.

I thought I was prepared, but on that day...

Freshly assigned to the royal guard, tasked with protecting Serafina at the Set Villa, I ran across a girl from my Zios Village days. Lyra lived in the neighboring village, and she knew about my real family and the happy days we spent together. No matter what I told myself, I couldn't bear to confront this physical proof of my past...and I fled like a scared rabbit.

Running away didn't bring me any relief. It only left me with deep regret and self-loathing. Crouched away in a back alley with my hands around my trembling knees, all I could think about was how small and pathetic I was.

It didn't help that later that night, the king spoke about the instability of the world. His story had an epic scope, spanning the ancient continent and the spirits—and he spoke of the only way to unravel a complex problem.

Normally, a story like that would have freaked me out, but weirdly enough, I got this sudden feeling like I had the answer. *No more running,* the thought pounded in me. *I became a knight to help people.*

So I ventured into Vlad Forest, brimming with the resolve to find the fruit the king instructed us he was looking for—only to discover that Lyra, the girl I was avoiding from my past, was working there as a saint.

None of us imagined that we'd wind up slaying monsters during our excursion to the villa, so we didn't bring any saints along. We hired a few saints from the local adventurers' guild for our journey into the forest, and Lyra just happened to be among them.

I felt her piercing gaze fixated on me, and I knew the time had finally come for me to confront my past.

This time, I would put my life on the line to protect the people.

But before that, I would have to come to terms with my wrongdoing. By acknowledging that it was my foolishness that brought death upon my family and neighbors, I could make a fresh start.

I won't screw up this time...

I called Lyra over, and we sat under a tree as I told her everything, every last sin. Although she lived in the neighboring village, she had friends and family who lived in Zios. I understood all too well how it felt to lose the people who were dear to you, and I fully expected her to hit me and scream at me.

But she didn't say a word of reproach. Instead, she cried and told me that she was glad that I was alive. It was like a bolt from the blue. All I could do was sit there, dumbfounded, as she gazed up at me with a tear-streaked face.

"Scheat, thank goodness you're still here."

She uttered those words from the heart—and in that instant, a gentle warmth trickled inside of me.

Ahh, I realized. She cared about me all this time. She didn't look coldly on me for what I did, for leading those monsters into the village. No, she was just happy to see me alive and well.

It did nothing to erase my crimes, but she was telling me that it was okay for me to be here. I bowed my head deeply to her and swore anew that I would use my life to save others. It was the least I could do to pay her back for her warm acceptance of me.

It took a while for my head to cool off after that. Then, as Lyra and I walked back to the others, she muttered softly...

"The monsters that attacked your village might still be in this forest."

Oh, right.

A shiver went down my spine.

On that fateful day twelve years ago, I lured monsters home from *this* forest. They probably returned here after they slaughtered the villagers, which meant that some of them might still be around to this day. How was I only realizing that now?

Damn it all. I couldn't stay calm after *that.* I had to exterminate every last monster in this forsaken forest.

As much as I knew that hunting the monsters here wouldn't bring back my family or the villagers, I was compelled to fight in their honor. My judgment clouded by dark thoughts, I made sure to finish off every monster I came across in Vlad Forest. I chased and cut down every last beast, even the ones that fled.

Miaplacidus told me to calm down, just like the people in the Sixth Knight Brigade did, but with all the blood rushing to my head, I couldn't heed his advice at all.

This went on for a few days until, out of nowhere, Lyra approached me and told me quietly, "Scheat, did you know that this forest has monsters you won't find anywhere else?"

Her expression was very grim. I could tell that she had worked herself up to tell me this, and that it wasn't just a fun fact.

"Just an hour's horse ride away from here, there's a coast with a cluster of large rocks. They say those rocks are the fragments of the ancient Lodrigone Continent, where plants, animals, and monsters were all different from what exists today. When those big rocks came ashore, they brought the ancient monsters along with them…and that's how they came to this land, they say."

"The monsters of Lodrigone…"

Every knight knew the stories. The ancient monsters were savagely violent—and cunning, to boot. Their physical abilities were on a different level from other monsters as well. They were supposed to have gone extinct after the continent disappeared, although some still lived on in very small numbers. Since they made their habitats in the deepest parts of the woods and very rarely showed up in front of people, they were feared as monsters of legend.

A bad feeling crept over me as I looked at Lyra.

"This forest is the closest to that rock cluster," she went on with a pallid face. "It's why they say the monsters of the Lodrigone Continent settled here. And one of those monsters is the ringed demon lion, a lion-type monster with ring-like patterns on its body."

"The ringed demon lion?" I frowned. I'd never heard of that one before.

"I'm not surprised you don't know about it," Lyra continued. "It's not a commonly used name, just a convenient nickname they use at the adventurers' guild. Very few have ever been slain, and there aren't many sightings of them either. The guild categorizes them as a variation on your regular demon lion."

Demon lions were two-meter-tall monsters that took on the shape of a lion. Although they packed quite a punch, their fighting patterns were straightforward, so they weren't too difficult for an experienced hand to slay.

"Everyone thinks the ringed demon lion is just another species of demon lion, not a monster of the Lodrigone Continent. But not too long ago, a team of knights came from the capital to survey the area, and they talked with the head of the adventurers' guild."

True to its name, the Eleventh Survey Knight Brigade was a knight brigade that researched monsters. Apparently, Lyra's uncle was in charge of the adventurers' guild, so she interacted with the knights as a kind of receptionist.

"They told me to keep my lips sealed, so I was hesitant to mention anything to you...but I think you deserve to know." Lyra lifted her downcast eyes and said, in a trembling tone, "Unlike other demon lions, the ringed demon lions walk on their hind legs."

If the ringed demon lion was a confirmed Lodrigone monster, she would absolutely have been sworn to secrecy about it. So why, despite knowing that, did she decide to go ahead and tell me?

"Being bipedal puts it a cut above your average lion-type monster, huh? Are you saying that's a Lodrigone monster trait?" I said lightly, trying to dispel the bad feeling churning inside me.

But Lyra answered with a straight face. "No, according to the survey knights, this monster's distinguishing trait is that... it's born without a shadow."

"What? No shadow?" That didn't sound real.

"Yes. They exist outside the bounds of this world's logic. To function here, they take on the shadow of the first living creature they kill."

My heart throbbed painfully in my chest.

"Apparently, the ringed demon lion is proud of the fact that it walks on two legs, so it would never take on the shadow of a four-legged beast. Now think about what two-legged creature lives in large enough numbers for them to target. The way it was explained to me, they have a habit of taking their freshly born offspring into the nearest village and...attacking every human on sight."

I couldn't form any words.

Pain split my head. Bile rose in my throat. I could have collapsed at any moment—that was how horrible I felt.

But I gritted my teeth, desperately forcing the feeling down, and concentrated on what Lyra was saying.

"So I...don't think it was your fault that Zios Village got attacked. Several ringed demon lions were born twelve years ago, and your village happened to be closest to Vlad Forest. That's all it was."

"Urk...!"

Good thing I skipped breakfast this morning. I might have puked out everything in my stomach.

But that didn't stop an awful cold sweat from running down my entire body. My heart raced unbearably. I clenched my chest and desperately tried to recall the tragedy from twelve years ago.

I must have caught a glimpse of the monsters that killed my family and the villagers. What did they look like?

Think. Remember.

I forced my way into the memories I'd blocked out of self-preservation.

Right...*right.* They were upright. The monsters were standing upright the whole time. I'd assumed my memories were wrong all along and suppressed them, because they were like no monsters I'd ever seen from Vlad Forest. But they were right there, in those memories I so desperately wanted to forget.

"Aaaaaaargh!"

My head sank, and my hands flew to my hair.

"How can this be?! They killed my family, they killed the villagers...and they took their shadows?!"

Not everyone's shadow got swiped, of course. The villagers far outnumbered the demon lions, so each monster would have killed multiple people. Not to mention that only the newborns could steal a person's shadow, and there could only have been so many of them.

But still, there was no question that the demon lions were behind the slaughter, which meant that *something* was traipsing around with the shadow of someone I once knew.

Lyra was looking at me in silence, but this was something I *had* to know. I peered up straight into her face.

"What happens to the person whose shape they steal? Are they still trapped inside the monster even after death?!"

Lyra blinked uneasily. "I...don't know," she said tremblingly. "But I heard that anyone familiar with the victim would recognize their silhouette in an instant."

Maybe the dead were beyond feeling anything. But even if it was only their appearance that lingered on, I still wanted to release them from being shackled to a monster in any way. I *had* to do it. It was the least I could do as a survivor—let it be my parting gift to them.

"Thanks. That was some valuable information."

The knight brigades had different areas of jurisdiction. If a Lodrigone monster were to appear, the Tenth Knight Brigade would take care of it since they were in charge of this western region. The job would never come to me, a member of Serafina's royal guard.

As I walked back to the others, brimming with resolve, Lyra called out behind me: "Scheat, the survey knights only came by because...because the adventurers have started sighting the ringed demon lions!"

It sounded as if she'd forced the words out of her throat. I raised a hand in lieu of a verbal response.

Adventurers generally didn't delve into a forest's depths unless they had a very good reason. If they were spotting Lodrigone monsters, it meant that the beasts were shrugging off their inhibitions and venturing out of their dens.

"Ha ha, so those monsters are looking to get their asses handed to them? I dunno what's got them sniffing around, but they ain't waltzing home alive, that's for sure."

The only reason I was able to talk so tough was because... I didn't know how terrifying the monsters of Lodrigone could be.

By strange coincidence, I encountered a group of ringed demon lions the very same day. I wasn't alone. Captain Deneb, who was stronger than me, was there, and so were Miaplacidus and Mirach. But even with our combined efforts, we only managed to take down one of the multiple demon lions that appeared.

About half of the beasts that got away had swollen bellies. They were getting ready for birth again.

Scheat's Resolve

IT TURNED OUT that Scheat's childhood friend Lyra was a saint who could help on the battlefield, and apparently, she joined the knights on their search of Vlad Forest. I could understand why she wanted to heal the unconscious Scheat herself, seeing as she would have fought alongside him and the other knights.

I looked at Scheat again, this time with a cool head. Only now did I realize that his injuries weren't life-threatening. *Lyra should handle this one,* I thought, stepping back.

Sirius swooped in and picked me up. "Good call," he said. "You've got a habit of overdoing it when you heal. Best to leave this one to her. Scheat's wounds might be serious, but you don't need to step in this time. What he needs is time to lie down and think."

I gazed at him in wonderment. As a saint, the only thing going through my head was healing Scheat right this instant, but Sirius had a broader view on things.

Glancing at the group that had returned from the forest, I noticed that there were a few other saints besides Lyra pitching in too. They'd even brought out their spirits, so I guess they had things under control.

Now what can I do? I jumped out of Sirius's arms when the answer came to me.

The knights were injured, but they were also drenched from the rain. I decided to help get their baths ready—if I were them, I'd want a nice, warm soak.

The knights looked refreshed after being healed, taking a bath, putting on a change of clothes, and getting some food in their bellies. Looking at them lounging around, I breathed a sigh of relief. Then my mind turned to Miaplacidus. I looked around the room and found him sitting on one of the sofas.

He noticed me timidly approaching. He also must have guessed what I was thinking from the look on my face, because I didn't even need to say anything before he immediately stood up and ushered me into a lounge room that no one else was using.

The moment he shut the door, the question I'd been dying to ask sprang out of my mouth. "How did Scheat get so hurt?"

Miaplacidus crouched in front of me. "There are monsters from the Lodrigone Continent dwelling in Vlad Forest," he explained calmly, "and today we encountered one of them, the ringed demon lion. They are an extremely powerful breed of monster, and they wounded many of our knights, Captain Deneb included. But the reason Scheat's wounds were so grievous is because he did not heed us when we told him to fall back. He charged at a monster all by himself."

"Monsters from the Lodrigone Continent" was new to me, so I blinked a few times in confusion when Miaplacidus mentioned them, but Scheat was the bigger concern on my mind. "Why was he being so reckless?" I asked.

Scheat might have looked like a free spirit, but he was actually a levelheaded knight who paid careful attention to his surroundings. There had to be a good reason why he lost his cool.

Miaplacidus hesitated for a bit. "Don't tell him I told you this," he said, before continuing, "Quite a few years ago, there was one time when Scheat got drunk out of his mind. I only found out later that he drank himself into a stupor because it was the anniversary of the day his village got attacked by monsters."

As bad as I felt about listening in on Scheat's secret, I nodded, wanting to hear more.

"He doesn't remember it himself, but he spilled a lot of truths that day. He used to be blond, but when his family and fellow villagers were slaughtered, his hair got drenched in their blood. The color's never gone away, and he kept insisting it was because he hadn't yet atoned for his crimes. He's still trapped by the past he hasn't been able to come to terms with."

Listening to Miaplacidus, I remembered what Sirius said about how Scheat's hometown was close by. "Maybe Scheat's village got attacked by monsters from Vlad Forest."

There weren't any other forests close by, after all. And since monsters lived in forests, you could assume that Vlad Forest was where the culprits came from, right?

Miaplacidus nodded slowly. He must have come to the same conclusion. "I think so too. I suspect he's trying to get revenge for his family and friends."

I fell silent, unsure of the right thing to say.

Miaplacidus looked straight at me, his face grim and serious. "If that's the case, I won't try to stop him," he went on. "If my friends and family were killed by monsters, slaying the culprits would be the only farewell gift I could imagine."

He spoke quietly, but there was something in his tone that made it impossible to argue with. Miaplacidus and Scheat both had their pride and convictions as knights. All I could do was nod, in awe of the way they lived their lives.

Miaplacidus and I left the room in silence.

Afterward, Lyra announced that she had finished healing Scheat. I thanked her and saw her off in the foyer.

She told me about Scheat. She said that she knew that his job was to guard me, and she didn't want me to have the wrong impression of him. From her, I learned about the ringed demon lion's special traits and how they were responsible for stealing the shadows of Scheat's family and fellow villagers.

"The monsters didn't just kill Scheat's family and friends, they also took their shadows..."

How terribly sad. When I visited Scheat in his room, I felt really heavy-hearted knowing that I couldn't do a single thing to erase the awful truth.

But he looked even sorrier than I felt. As he pulled an apologetic face, he lifted his still-wounded body from the bed. "I'm so sorry for worrying you, Princess Serafina. I can't apologize enough for my blunder. Ha ha, who knew I'd get beaten senseless? Shows how much I've still got to learn."

Scheat smiled brightly as if to cheer me up, which only made me feel worse.

"Scheat, Lyra told me about the monsters. And your hometown and family," I said bluntly.

Scheat's expression clouded over. He covered his face with both hands, and when he spoke, his voice was shakier than I'd ever heard it before. "I suppose you *are* my liege. You deserve to know. But...I didn't want *anyone* to know what a sniveling, cowering wreck I was for twelve years."

I hurriedly sidled up to Scheat and took his arm. "I don't think you're like that at all! You've always been cool and dependable to me!"

Scheat kept his face buried in his hands for a while until finally he seemed to have made a decision. He pulled his hands away forcefully.

Then he lifted his face and looked me in the eyes.

"No, Your Highness, I *am* pathetic. I needed someone less than half my age to comfort me."

I'd never seen such a miserable face in my life. Even if some people were to call it "pathetic," I shook my head firmly. "You're too cool, Scheat!" I insisted.

Scheat frowned and looked moodily toward the window. "You must've heard about the demon lions with the ringed patterns. It was news to me too... I only heard about them today, and then I actually bumped right into them. Can you believe that? They walk on their hind legs...and they have human shadows."

The rain continued to pour.

"It's rainy and cloudy out, so I bet there's no moonlight tonight," he said, not looking away. "You wouldn't see any shadows on a night like this. You think my friends who lost their shadows are having a moment of peace right now?"

Scheat looked like he was about to cry. His mouth clenched shut, and he stared up into the pitch-black world outside. He always had such a vibrant appearance, but when his face twisted in uncertainty like this, he looked so terribly fragile.

Thinking that I had to do *something* to cheer him up, I said, "Scheat, your wounds were so bad that Lyra even said she couldn't heal them all. You gotta stay in bed for two or three days. In the meantime, why don't you have a nice long think about what you want to do?"

Looking at Scheat again, I noticed that he had a shirt strewn over his upper body, but he hadn't buttoned it up at all, leaving all the bandages around his chest and stomach in plain sight.

Although I felt bad for Scheat, I could tell that Lyra had done a great job by only patching him up halfway. I would have healed him up completely, and then he would have picked up his sword and marched straight back to Vlad Forest. He would have gotten badly hurt again for sure.

Scheat wasn't being his usual self. I could tell that he needed time to stop and think things through. A full heal wasn't always the right answer, just like Sirius said.

As I was gazing at Scheat's wounds, he put a hand over the bandages on his chest and gritted his teeth. "I don't need all that downtime! This is nothing. I can go back and slay monsters tomorrow, no sweat!"

"Huuuh? Wh-what are you saying? You got hurt real bad and you're still covered in wounds! You can't fight like that!"

He made no sense. The way it looked to me, he'd received just the right amount of healing, but did he need *more* wounds to keep him in bed?

As I was staring wide-eyed at Scheat, he clenched his fist and put on a determined face. "I don't need time to think. I already know what I want to do."

"I-I'm sure you do! So, um...what *do* you want to do?" I asked nervously.

He looked back at me without a second of hesitation. "I'm gonna beat every last demon lion who destroyed my village myself!" he declared.

The intensity in his voice told me that if there was a monster in the room, he would have sprung at it immediately.

"What? B-but, um..."

I heard they'd only managed to take down one demon lion today—and Scheat still came out of it with big wounds. I didn't know how many ringed demon lions there were out there, but Scheat definitely couldn't handle them all by himself.

I still kind of understood what Scheat was feeling, though, so I couldn't bring myself to say that he was wrong. I just looked back at him in silence.

His mouth twisted into a grimace. "Aww, don't look like that. Even I know my limits."

He covered his eyes with his hands.

"Darn it!" His voice sounded lower than usual. "I wish I had unlimited strength! What I'd give to take down those demon lions myself! I bet Vice-Commander Sirius could handle them... but *I* want to be the one to do it. I know it's selfish of me. It'd take me years to do it myself, and that would just mean more suffering for everyone who had their shadows stolen. I don't want them trapped another day. And besides...I found another reason to hurry. There'll be more victims soon if we wait around."

I could see that Scheat was struggling with a lot of different emotions, so I tried making an obvious suggestion. "Um, how about fighting with Sirius? He can weaken them and you can finish them off!"

Scheat grimaced. "That would be nice, but their hides are tough. It's not easy landing a killing blow. Vice-Commander Sirius can lop off a monster's head in one strike, but that's not something any ordinary knight can do."

"Oh, um, is that right?" I frowned, surprised that there was such a wide gap between Sirius and the other knights. What was Scheat supposed to do, then?

Scheat put a hand to his hair and said in a pained voice, "Slaying monsters isn't the royal guard's job in the first place. We went into the forest to search for something and just happened to encounter the demon lions. Now that I'm all beat up like this, I'm sure the vice-commander is gonna call everything off. So..."

Oh no.

It sounded like Scheat was about to say "I'm going to quit the royal guard." Or even worse, "I'm resigning as a knight."

As I was opening my mouth in a frantic attempt to stop him, a familiar voice rang out first.

"You would be correct in that assumption. I *am* calling off the search tomorrow."

When I swung around, Sirius was leaning against the door.

◇ ◇ ◇

"Wha—? S-Sirius..." My tongue tripped over his name.

I went up to Sirius, wanting him to take back his words. He patted me on the head reassuringly before turning his head back to Scheat.

"Scheat, I heard you were playing fast and loose with your life, and that seems to be the truth from what I can see of your injuries. Has losing all that blood stopped it from rushing to your head?"

Scheat's face twisted in shame. He sat up straight and bowed his head. "I'm so sorry about all the trouble I caused, Vice-Commander! My recklessness got everyone hurt! But I—"

Sirius interrupted him. "I just got a report from the Eleventh Knight Brigade. They identified the carcass you guys brought in from Vlad Forest as a Lodrigone monster."

Scheat's eyes widened.

"The ringed demon lion was first identified in a different region, and most of its traits and abilities have already been analyzed," Sirius went on. "The Survey Knight Brigade has been investigating whether the same monster exists in Vlad Forest, based on recent reports from the adventurers' guild."

Sirius cut himself off there and glanced at Scheat's face. He seemed satisfied that Scheat was following along, and so he continued.

"I have bad news for you. The report says that the ringed demon lions become aggressive around the time they give birth. It's only been twelve years since the last time, but the whole pride is now on the prowl again. They're all moving out from the forest's depths in search of two-legged creatures... I suspect that might be why the local palace lord is holing himself up."

Scheat ground his teeth audibly, but Sirius simply folded his arms in thought.

"There's no ambiguity here. Deneb told me that the demon lions you ran into had swollen bellies. There's a significant risk they'll attack *another* nearby village soon. We don't have much time."

Scheat's face shot up the moment those words left Sirius's mouth. "Vice-Commander Sirius!" he screamed. "The Royal Red Shield is a team of hand-picked elites. We've got a better shot of this than anyone! Please order us to exterminate the ringed demon lions!"

Sirius shot Scheat a penetrating look. "The Survey Knight Brigade estimates that, based on the attack on Zios Village, there are around thirty ringed demon lions in total. That's a considerable number. Do you really think that you can take on the monsters of Lodrigone with just the knights here?"

Scheat's eyebrows furled into a thunderous frown. He threw a sharp look at Sirius, but his lips remained shut. It was because he knew from fighting the demon lions for himself just how strong they were. I could tell from Scheat's face that thirty was a higher number than he expected.

Knowing that he couldn't easily say "yes" to the question, Scheat started talking about his past instead. "Vice-Commander, I'm a survivor of the Zios Village attack from twelve years ago! Those monsters killed my friends and family! And not just that, they took their shadows! The people I knew are still captive to this day!"

Sirius said nothing to interject. He listened to Scheat in silence.

"I defeated a demon lion today. When it died, its shadow detached from its body and rose into the sky. I watched it curl its pointer finger and bring its hands together. That's a sign of prayer in Zios Village. I think the shadow belonged to the local landlady who always made me bread." The desperation was plain in Scheat's voice. "Maybe I was just seeing what I wanted to see, but the landlady's shadow looked so happy to me when it ascended! I want to free them all by my own hand—my family, the villagers, even strangers. Everyone!"

Sirius unfolded his arms and strode to the bed, gazing straight down at Scheat. Scheat met his gaze, his eyes fiery with resolve.

He clenched his trembling hands into fists. "I know I'm just making an emotional argument! The knights are my friends too—I don't want a single one of them to get hurt because of my recklessness! If you make an objective analysis and decide we're not up to the task, I'll respect it."

Silence ensued.

Then, after what felt like an eternity, the corner of Sirius's lips lifted. "Now that's what I like to hear. Shall we gear up for battle, then?"

"Wait, whaaat?" Sirius's words must have been so unexpected that Scheat's voice squeaked from all the tension. I'd never heard that sound out of his mouth before. Then he started blinking furiously as the meaning of what Sirius said settled in.

Sirius put a hand on Scheat's shoulder. "It's good to have emotions. They give you purpose and strength. Make no mistake—the knights and I will focus on wearing down the monsters and *you* will land the finishing blow."

"Wh-what? You're...okay with that?!" Scheat was taken aback. He looked like he was desperately trying to get his thoughts in order. "There's thirty of them, and you just said you called off the search in the forest. I thought the plan was to—"

"Exterminate the Lodrigone monsters, not search the forest," Sirius drawled. "I did not misspeak."

He flashed a grin in response to Scheat's slack-jawed expression.

He then barked at the hallway: "No objections?!"

"None, sir!"

A throng of voices rang out within a second. Startled, I looked over my shoulder and saw a bunch of knights standing outside the open door. At some point, they'd all gathered in the hallway. Everyone looked like they were on board with Sirius's command. The only person who seemed to have been out of the loop was Scheat.

"B-but, Vice-Commander Sirius!" he shouted shakily, a look of utter disbelief on his face. "Isn't it a bit much for *me* to land the finishing bl—?"

"You might not have noticed this, but I deeply revere Serafina. This is *her* strategy, and we can't go against the princess's orders, now can we?"

Scheat finally seemed to realize that Sirius's plan was the exact same thing I'd suggested a moment ago. He grimaced. "Vice-Commander, I'm well aware of your partiality to the princess," was all he said. This was his way of saying that he accepted the plan.

Sirius cracked a small smile as Scheat put his hands on the bed and bowed his head deeply. "Thank you so much, Vice-Commander Sirius! Princess Serafina! And all of you as well!"

I thought the knights would be stunned into silence at Scheat acting so serious...but they were the complete opposite.

"Ha ha, good for you, Scheat!" The voices boomed down the corridor.

"But you didn't need to say that rubbish about 'if we're not up to the task!'" another knight added teasingly. "We ain't weaklings!"

"Heal this man up already!" Miaplacidus called out.

"Oh, right," Sirius muttered, as if that had slipped his mind entirely.

This small reaction seemed to cause a ripple among the knights, because they all stopped moving and turned their attention to him.

Meanwhile, Sirius pulled out a small bottle from his breast pocket and chucked it at Scheat. "Drink this before bed. Your wounds should be gone by morning."

"What?"

"The battle is tomorrow! I expect everyone to be in tip-top shape!" Sirius announced before picking me up and marching out of the room. After a momentary silence, a round of cheers sounded from behind him.

Sirius chuckled in amusement at the war cries. "Ha ha ha, looks like everyone's raring to take down the Lodrigone monsters. Gallant indeed." He sounded super, super proud.

Sirius really loves the knights, I thought, feeling all warm and fuzzy inside.

As I clung to his neck, he turned to look at me. "Serafina, thanks for sticking with Scheat. You're a fine liege. And I have to hand it to you for making an instant recovery potion. Curing such severe wounds is no easy feat for a saint."

Sirius gave Scheat a healing potion I made specially for him. It was strong enough to patch up even old wounds like new.

"Tee hee hee! You're a really great knight, so I gotta be super good to keep up with you!" I praised him back. I knew he was just saying that because he was in a good mood, but his compliments still made me happy.

"Ha ha ha!" He laughed in pure delight. "You said it!"

"Yep, I sure did!"

That's how we spent the night before the battle—joyously happy.

A Tale of the Secret Saint ZERO

INTERLUDE

Preparing for Battle (Huh? *She's* Coming Too?!)

EARLY THE NEXT MORNING, as the knights were preparing for their departure, Serafina emerged into the living room at a time when she would normally have still been asleep. Because she was in an adorable green dress, they all assumed that she had come to see them off, but…

"Here already, Serafina? That's a nice dress, looks good on you… So I assume that you woke up early to come with us?" asked Sirius.

Serafina gave a cheerful answer. "Yep!"

"Say whaaaaat?!"

The knights' astonished shouts were understandable. Their efforts were entirely concentrated on defeating the Lodrigone monsters; none of them thought themselves capable of juggling this with their guard duties.

At the same time, being knights of the Royal Red Shield, they were obligated to prioritize Serafina under any and all circumstances. They also knew that today's mission was outside the regular confines of their duty, and that Sirius had graciously allowed Scheat to realize his wishes. If Sirius, who clearly doted on Serafina, allowed her to accompany them, they would have to fall in line.

At this point, Serafina had yet to unequivocally demonstrate her talents as a saint to the knights. They had no idea that she would be lending battle support, and nobody had bothered to inform them. The knights quickly smothered their undignified outburst with steely expressions, and so Serafina failed to notice that they were laboring under a misunderstanding.

Sirius, on the other hand, *did* notice. He had already explained that Serafina was a saint, so he was puzzled by the knights' reactions. He wasn't disposed to repetition and had never encountered any problems issuing clear and concise information.

Nevertheless, the knights' reactions bothered him. "Serafina will be participating as a saint," he said, just in case they weren't on the same page. "I don't know what the other saints are doing today. Are the ones from yesterday available?"

"Yes, they are!" Captain Deneb answered. "I consulted with the adventurers' guild yesterday about today's mission. The guild master said that they don't have anyone better than the five saints that are already dispatched. I expect that their performance will take a hit from working consecutive days, but it's the best lineup we've got."

Inwardly, Captain Deneb questioned whether Princess Serafina would be up to snuff as a saint, but he wisely chose not to let that thought show on his face.

"Sirius, if the other saints are tired from fighting every day, should I bring some of my healing potions?" said Serafina.

"That would be a good idea," said Sirius.

"Then I'll make my special 'get well' potion with honey!"

This prompted the knights to mutter inwardly:

"Oh, is that the thing she made for Canopus?"

"Serafina has a habit of putting honey into everything. It's the thought that counts, but I suppose she doesn't know that mixing in different ingredients messes up a potion's effects."

"But hey, she is our princess. It's nice of her to make healing potions—well, nutritional supplements—for us."

Then, without exception, the knights turned their eyes to Serafina's hands. Only now, after Serafina claimed to make a healing potion and Sirius vouched for her, did they find themselves curious about whether this little princess was actually a saint. It was common knowledge that when a saint made a pact with a spirit, a sigil would appear on the backs of their hands. The intensity of this sigil's color indicated the strength of the contracted spirit—hence why the knights glanced in that direction.

When they saw that neither of her hands had a sigil, they shrugged inwardly. *"Figures,"* they thought. As far as they knew, spirits only formed pacts with adult women, and their princess was a scant six years of age.

"By 'saint,' Vice-Commander Sirius might be referring to anyone who can make healing potions, in which case Princess Serafina will run out of magic almost immediately."

"Either way...it takes real guts for such a tiny princess to accompany us into a forest with Lodrigone monsters."

"A princess this plucky is bound to become a great saint in the future."

The knights collectively diverted their optimism to the future.

The Monsters of the Lodrigone Continent

"SERAFINA, THAT DRESS doesn't seem easy to walk in," Sirius said as he picked me up.

"Oh no, Sirius! You'll fighting a whole lot, so you shouldn't use up your strength now! I'm fine—don't you worry about me!" I said, wriggling my legs.

But Sirius just smiled like he thought it was funny. "Ha ha ha, if carrying you around was a drain on my stamina, I'd be a disgrace of a knight."

I saw no hint of him letting me down anytime soon, so I decided to stop struggling. Best not to make him use up any more stamina. I felt bad about my choice of dress, though. Oligor had said it would bring good luck, but Sirius had a point: It wasn't good for walking around in a forest.

While I was down in the dumps, Sirius had a cheeky grin on his face. "What's wrong? Tired because you got out of bed earlier than usual? By all means, take a nap. I'll wake you when the monsters show up."

Oh, jeez! Who did Sirius think I was? I'd never nod off in a forest crawling with monsters.

As I grumbled on the inside, Sirius squeezed me in his hold. "I'm just grateful you're here."

I turned toward him, wondering what he was talking about.

There was an uneasy frown on his face. "I told the king that I would only bring you to the battlefield after you've had training and I've deemed you ready. Today, I'm breaking my promise to him, but...I swear I'll protect you. Hide behind me if you feel even a hint of fear."

Oh dear, was Sirius still worried about such a silly thing? "I won't hide! Not unless I'm in the way!"

"Oh, so you intend to fight the whole time? You'd better take a quick magic restoration potion if you need one. I very much doubt we'll defeat all the ringed demon lions today. I intend to pull back when we've made a decent amount of progress, but you might run out of magic before then, so..."

Sirius trailed off there, perhaps because he was thinking about that one time we fought together. Back then, I was the only saint supporting a big group of knights, but I was never close to running out of magic. To be fair, though, the knights were hardly scratched, so I had a lot of magic in reserve.

A deer-type monster jumped out from the bushes, interrupting my thoughts.

Sirius swiftly placed me at his feet and said, "Stay near me so you don't get swiped up by a monster again." He was talking about that time not too long ago when a griffon kidnapped me while I was watching him fight from afar.

The knights told me and the other saints beforehand that our help would only be needed during the ringed demon lion fight, so we sat out for now. At first, I thought that the demon lions had to be terrifying if the saints had to preserve their magic, but when I saw how easily the knights took out the five deer monsters, I realized what they *really* meant. They were so strong that they didn't need the saints' help. Oopsies, should've picked up on that.

It was my first time seeing my royal guard fight, so I just didn't know just how good they were. As I marveled over them, it occurred to me that I simply *had* to tell them what I was feeling.

"Wow! Amazing!" I gushed. "Father said the royal guard's biggest job was looking cool, but you're all super strong!"

I had a feeling they were strong when Sirius first introduced me to them, but then I got confused when Father declared that their looks outweighed their strength. Now that I was actually seeing them fight, though, my heart swelled with pride.

I meant what I said as praise, but for some reason it made the knights scowl. Later on, Captain Deneb spoke for everyone when he said, "We are honored by His Majesty's words," but he didn't look happy in the slightest.

Hmm, I was trying to say that their strength took me by surprise in a nice way, but if that didn't get through, how was I supposed to tell them?

We encountered a few other monsters after that, but the knights took care of them all without breaking a sweat. What a surprise—it hit me all over again that Sirius had picked an incredible team.

◇◇◇

"Sirius, is this forest special?" I asked.

I noticed we'd been using the same type of tree as a sort of guidepost ever since we entered the forest.

"Good eye," Sirius praised me. "This is called a shira tree. They produce a special aroma, which our demon lions are very attracted to. The pride as a whole is headed for the forest's entrance, but they always stop by these trees on the way. So if we go deeper into the forest using these trees as checkpoints, we're bound to bump into each other at some point."

"That makes sense," I said idly as I cast a casual glance at Scheat. He looked very tense, which worried me. "Scheat's been so nervous this whole time. Is he gonna be okay?" I whispered to Sirius.

"Mm. He's been using an excessive amount of energy in these past few fights. But I can't say I blame him. He's trying to let go of a burden he's been carrying for a long time. Serafina, keep an eye on Scheat when you're not too distracted in battle. If anyone's likely to go overboard and put himself at risk, it's him."

"Got it!" I said with a brave face, although I had to wonder whether I'd be able to keep track of so many things at once. It was nice that Sirius relied on me, though.

Turning my attention to him, I realized that *he* looked nervous too.

"What's the matter, Sirius?" I asked in surprise.

He was quiet for a moment before he solemnly spoke. "They're still some distance away, but I suspect that there's a group of our targets ahead. Even if they're not the monsters we're looking for, they're an extremely strong bunch."

"What?!"

I was surprised that Sirius was quicker to notice the monsters' presence. One of the knights had magic and was in charge of searching for the enemy, but it didn't look like he'd noticed what Sirius had.

Before I could recover from my shock, Captain Deneb shouted at everyone to get ready—he must have overheard us. As I watched the knights shift from a search formation to a battle one, a surge of tension ran through me. I could tell that these monsters were a much bigger threat than all the others we'd encountered.

My heart raced in my chest, feeling like it was about to burst from all the throbbing. Meanwhile, the other saints called for their spirits. Oh right, I had to summon Seven! Just as I was about to climb out of Sirius's arms, he crouched and lowered me to the ground.

"Serafina, wait for three minutes after the battle starts before you do anything."

"Huh?!"

Three minutes was a long time in a battle. Was it really a good idea for me to stay put for that long? What for?

My confusion must have shown on my face, because Sirius answered, “The knights need to experience how strong the monsters are for their future reference. They’d lose the capacity to gauge their own strength and their opponent’s strength if you were to jump in from the start.”

“Y-you have a point!” I agreed with a nod.

Sirius smiled, pulled out his sword, and readied it in front of him.

Yeah, he was right. The other saints knew when to cast the right spells for the situation, but I didn’t have much experience. I was bound to cast a load of buffs right at the start, which would improve the knights’ abilities beyond their recognition.

Seven once told me that the same spell would have a different impact depending on the caster, and the same differences probably existed between the knights. This meant that it was important for them to know how strong they were compared to the monsters without the saints’ support.

“Well, *of course* I don’t know a thing about battle! I have a lot to learn!” I said sheepishly.

When I lifted my head, Canopus was standing in front of me. I looked behind myself in surprise, and Mirach was there with his back to me. Ah, so they were protecting me. I felt bad about taking up two valuable party members when a big battle was about to begin.

I looked around and saw that the other saints had already gotten behind the knights.

"Sorry, I'll go straight to the rear! I'll be safe, and you two can focus on the monsters!"

I rushed over to the other saints, but for some reason Canopus and Mirach followed me.

Uh-oh! Maybe they saw I was in danger before, and now they were unwilling to leave me alone.

In that same instant, a sharp voice rang through the scene. "They're here!"

Startled, I turned my gaze directly ahead—just as five demon lions appeared.

Unlike the pictures in the encyclopedia, these stood on thick hind legs. And as they drew closer, the ring-like patterns on their bodies came into view.

A shiver ran down my spine. So this was a monster of the Lodrigone Continent—the difference from a regular demon lion was plain to see. Now that knew I was seeing the ringed demon lions in the flesh, I could sense a vicious and menacing aura from each and every one of them. They were a full head taller than our beefiest knights, and their fangs, claws, and tails glinted with sharp edges.

But despite their monstrous forms, the shadows that fell to the ground were all human-shaped.

Oh my goodness! They really did trap people in their shadows! I couldn't blame Scheat, Mirach, and Miaplacidus at all for wanting to slay the monsters and release the trapped victims.

"Urgh, seeing their shadows makes me sick! How dare they think they can keep getting away with killing people and stealing their shadows! Time to show these bastards that humans aren't pushovers!" Scheat roared as he readied his sword and charged at a demon lion.

Maybe he was nervous, because his movements looked a little stiff to me. That was probably why the demon lion smoothly dodged when Scheat swung his sword down. He took a step forward and swung another two times, but none of his hits landed.

The knights won very easily against all the other monsters we'd encountered in the forest, but it was the total opposite with the ringed demon lions.

But Scheat didn't give up. He kept on swinging until finally his sword sank into the monster's body. Unfortunately, he didn't get it in very far, so the monster only ended up with a slight cut.

"Oh no! Their hides are so thick!" Who would have imagined they'd stop Scheat's sword? His arms were so muscular *and* he was super skilled!

Scheat's slash was the cue for a bunch of other knights to jump into the fray, but this battle didn't play out like the others. None of their swords cut deep enough to cause a fatal wound. I clenched my hands tightly and started a desperate count.

Twenty-three, twenty-four, twenty-five...

As the ineffective slashes kept mounting, Sirius stood out as the only exception. Surprisingly, his sword cut deep, like it was made out of a completely different metal from all the others. Blood spewed whenever he buried his blade into a demon lion's body and yanked it back out. The knights scattered around him were all moving and swinging their swords in the same way, so what made their cuts so shallow?

They seemed to be getting flustered, and their moves got visibly shakier as time passed. Just then, Sirius approached the biggest demon lion in the group and buried his blade into it with a brilliant, rapid stroke of his sword.

As the monster's blood went spraying, Sirius howled, "Get a grip on yourselves! Is this the best you can do?! I taught you differently! Don't bother conserving your strength—put everything you have into each strike!"

For an instant, everyone's eyes widened in surprise, but then they all clenched their swords. Someone let out a deep breath, and someone else thumped their chest... They all had different ways of psyching themselves up. When they were done, they threw themselves at the demon lions once more.

Their newfound motivation must have quickened their movements or improved the weight of their strikes, because now their swords were cutting deeper. They'd turned into completely different fighters in a mere instant.

I gawked at the sight. "Wow! Sirius isn't just a great swordsman, he's a brilliant commander too!" Just a word from his lips restored the knights' morale and made them tap into a new reserve of strength.

But even that wasn't enough to bring down their foes. The monsters of Lodrigone weren't going down without a fight. Even as the knights buried their blades into the monsters, they were getting bitten and clawed in return. Large gashes opened up on their arms and torsos, causing blood to splatter the scene.

Not a single knight retreated to the back lines, though. In fact, they advanced a step further and pelted their foes with powerful strikes. The knights had strength in numbers, and they used that to their advantage. Multiple knights ganged up on each monster and whittled down its strength.

Meanwhile, Sirius fought one of the beasts all by himself, and he clearly had the upper hand. A powerful swing of his sword lopped off a demon lion's arm. As the beast howled in pain, Sirius made a follow-up slash across its stomach.

"Scheat!" Sirius shouted over his shoulder, just as the monster collapsed.

Scheat instantly came running. His eyes burned with hatred for the demon lion on the ground. The next moment, however, his gaze shifted to what was at his feet—the monster's all-too-human shadow.

"I'll free you now!" Scheat declared as he gripped his sword in both hands and ran it through the monster's heart.

When he pulled out the blade, blood went flying and gushing everywhere. As the blood rained, the black shadow seemed to separate itself from the monster and rise into the sky.

I watched with bated breath as the shadow turned its head around hesitantly, gazing down at the demon lion it was no longer a part of. Then it turned to Scheat and did a little bow, as if it was showing its thanks.

Scheat gasped, and a visible tremble ran through his body. But the shadow turned its head up to the sky and floated straight up, not looking back.

"We...freed a person," Scheat muttered as he curled his pointer finger and did the prayer sign of his village.

The shadow didn't do the same unique prayer sign as Scheat, so it might not have been a resident of Zios.

Regardless, Scheat still looked as if a slight weight had been lifted off his shoulders.

◇ ◇ ◇

"We're not done yet, Scheat! Everyone else, follow the vice-commander's lead! We're taking down those monsters!" Captain Deneb's energetic voice roared.

"Yes, sir!" the knights roared back dutifully.

Meanwhile, Scheat adjusted the grip on his sword and lunged at another demon lion.

I focused on counting as I followed the scene with my eyes.

Eighty-one, eighty-two, eighty-three...

Although the knights had definitely worn down the monsters, their injuries were clearly increasing too. I bet that Lyra and the other saints were worn out from the multiple days of fighting, which meant that their spells had a shorter range. With them standing well out of the way of the terrifying Lodrigone monsters, their healing magic had no way of reaching the knights.

But me? I had plenty of magic to spare from reading picture books in my room all day. I bet my magic could reach every inch of the battlefield, even from where I was standing.

Eighty-nine, ninety, ninety-one...

A monster sank its claws into Scheat's shoulder.

Miaplacidus tried to help Scheat by brandishing his sword at the beast, but then a new demon lion jumped in from an unexpected direction, baring its fangs. The nearby knights instantly swooped in for the attack, but not before it tore a chunk out of Miaplacidus's arm.

"Tch!" Miaplacidus grunted at his blunder and switched his sword to his other hand. It looked like he couldn't use his dominant hand anymore.

The other knights stopped their attack, wary of how a monster had shown up seemingly out of nowhere. Their eyes soon fell on an unexpected sight: Ten new ringed demon lions had emerged from the forest's depths.

The knights gaped in astonishment. The remaining four demon lions were enough to give them trouble. With three times the number of foes, there was no way the knights could keep up. They started to back down so that they could regroup.

But the demon lions closed in one step at a time, unrelenting. To make matters worse, more of them continued to appear one after another. Soon, they would completely encircle us.

"Urk, the survey knights were off the mark! They said the monsters moved in groups of five, but we're up against the whole pride!" Mirach spat behind me.

By the time the knights finished regrouping so that they were surrounding me and the other saints, there were more than thirty demon lions.

"We hadn't accounted for this! There's no way we can fight through this many of them! Continuing the mission is futile! Dang it, we're surrounded. Ugh, the bigger question is how many of us can slip away?"

Mirach had already given up on slaying the demon lions and was talking about retreat. I looked up at him in shock. Sure, there were a lot of monsters, but we had Sirius, and the other knights were super strong as well. I thought we stood a chance with the help of supporting magic.

Up till now, the knights had all been taking the fight to the monsters, putting them out of range of the saints' magic—but now they were clustered around the saints. Lyra and the others could cast their spells on everyone here.

"Mirach," I called out.

"Don't you fear, Princess Serafina. I won't let you suffer a scratch," Mirach replied, his eyes trained on the monsters.

That wasn't what I was trying to say. I was about to mention that I could fight too.

But maybe Mirach was right and I was underestimating the demon lions.

One hundred and thirteen, one hundred and fourteen, one hundred and fifteen...

I kept on counting desperately.

I had to be patient. Sirius had given me his command because he was taking into account not just this battle but future ones as well. Patience was key. Then again, maybe I could pretend I messed up my counting?

But the next moment, I stopped counting anyway—because all thirty-plus monsters attacked at once, and some of them were headed straight my way.

My eyes widened. At my front and behind, Canopus and Mirach readied their swords to protect me.

The monsters that came lunging at us must have been really heavy, because when Mirach stopped one with his sword, his legs couldn't support him and he fell to one knee. The harsh screech of metal against claw rang out.

Although Canopus managed to fend off his foe, blood dripped down his cheek where the monster's claws had scratched it.

The saints screamed in terror at this first-hand display of the demon lions' savagery. They sank to the ground, having lost the will to fight. Their spirits looked down at them worriedly, but unless the saints cast a spell, all they could really do was float there in the air.

Even though the saints must have ventured into this forest with adventurers countless times, they had succumbed to fear. The knights, however, didn't show a speck of uncertainty as they faced off against the monsters. They readied their swords, still in the fight. Blood spurted from their wounds, but nobody retreated. The way they stubbornly held their ground was honestly very dashing.

When I glanced at Scheat, I saw that he was panting heavily. Despite that, there was still an unwaveringly strong gleam in his eyes. I didn't get the impression that he was backing down anytime soon.

Seeing everyone fight so valiantly, I clasped my hands together—and at that moment, a nasty tearing sound rang out behind me.

Startled, I looked over my shoulder, only to find that Mirach had been clawed by a monster in an attempt to defend me.

"Mirach!" I cried.

But even though blood spurted from his chest, Mirach's expression didn't so much as flicker. "It's just a scratch. But it looks like we're in a spot of danger. You and Canopus should retreat. I'll secure an escape route for you."

I was just about to respond when I noticed Sirius dashing toward me. "Serafina!"

Even though he should have been taking command of the knights, he came for me because he was worried.

"Sirius!" I hurried over to him.

He scooped me up with his free hand, and his eyes quickly swept over me, softening when he saw that I was unhurt.

A tense look soon came over his face, though. "This is the worst-case scenario that I accounted for; it's gotten too messy for a beginner. Retreat with Canopus and Mirach."

"What?!"

"I know your talents, but it's too risky for you to be here. The situation's gotten bad enough that I need to focus on getting the knights out of here alive. Protecting you at the same time will be tricky. I'm sorry about breaking my promise, but my top priority is getting you out of here first. I'll catch up with you later."

I understood what Sirius was trying to say; it took way more effort to defend a powerless person like me than support a group of skilled swordsmen. With the situation so out of control, he wanted me out of the way, just in case worse came to worst. He would never tell me to heal the knights if it meant putting myself in harm's way.

As touched as I was by his kindness, frustration boiled inside me. I wasn't doing what I had come here to do. So many knights were injured, and I was supposed to help them!

"N-n-no!"

When I noticed that Sirius was trying to hand me off to Canopus, I desperately twisted my body and tumbled out of Sirius's arms.

"Serafina?!"

"I came here to protect the knights! And I waited the whole three minutes!" I stopped counting somewhere along the line, so I wasn't actually sure if three minutes had passed, but I said so with confidence anyway. "So give me three minutes—no, one minute! Thirty seconds!"

It was going to be hard for me to support all the knights by myself when the other saints had lost the will to fight.

But I knew that I could do *something* to turn the tides.

As soon as the words were out of my mouth, I threw my head toward the sky. I was going to do everything I could do before Sirius stopped me.

"Come to me, Seven!" I called out in the spirit language.

Seven instantly appeared before me. *"Oh, here you are, Fi! I was wondering where you went off to so early in the morning. You're not much of an early bird, you...knooooooooow?!"*

He started that sentence all blasé and cheerful, but his voice turned funny when he caught sight of all the bleeding knights.

Hurriedly, he scanned the surroundings. *"What the—?"* His eyes widened as he pointed at a ringed demon lion. *"Is that a monster from the ancient continent? What the heck have you been up to?!"*

Although he was clearly exasperated, he still flew high in the sky and started channeling his spirit powers into me. The pact sigil on the backs of my hands instantly came into view—the same bright red color as my hair.

When I was certain that Seven's power had converted into my magic, I held a hand up into the sky. Then, as I swept my eyes across the knights on the field, I chanted a spell.

"Heal!"

It was just one word—but it did everything.

In the blink of an eye, all the knights' injuries disappeared and their missing bits of flesh returned.

"Huh?"

"What?!"

"'Scuse meeee?!"

The knights gazed in astonishment at their fully healed bodies, but then they turned their heads up and gawked at me.

"Is...Princess Serafina an actual saint?!"

"No kidding?!"

"Is it even possible for a spell to cover this much ground?!"

Right in front of me, Mirach was also staring down at his formerly slashed chest in astonishment.

The cool and collected Canopus was wide-eyed for a moment. "Impossible... She targeted so many people and yet *still* managed such thorough healing?" he breathed shakily.

Further along the battlefield, Miaplacidus silently switched his sword back to his dominant hand. Scheat threw me a look of surprise, but then he turned to face one of the demon lions again. He gripped his sword, looking hungry for battle.

Once I was confident that everyone was healed, I cast a supporting spell.

"Invigorate! Attack ×1.5; Speed ×1.5!"

Since the demon lions' hides were too tough for the knights to cut through, I made sure the spell was stronger than usual.

I then cast an uncertain look at all the demon lions on the scene. There was another spell I wanted to use. Normally, I would have tested it out first since I was still practicing it, but Oligor promised my dress would bring me good fortune, so I had a feeling things might go my way.

"Please, O Blessed Dress of the Spirits, give me luck!" I didn't forget to ask nicely first.

Then I spread my arms out toward the demon lions.

"Unseen chains, grow stout and ensnare that which lies before me! Bind!"

The moment I finished my chant, chains of light appeared over the monsters' heads. They wrapped around their targets with blinding speed, but I was only able to fully restrain three demon lions. I did manage to partially tie down some of the others' arms and feet, but only about ten of them. The rest of them swerved nimbly out of the way.

"Phooey, even with the spirits' blessing, was this all I could do? I gotta practice more."

It was depressing, but then I remembered that this wasn't the time or place to mope, so I hurriedly looked back to the battle.

"Oh, that was already thirty seconds! I guess I should run away with Canopus and Mirach now, huh?"

But even though Sirius and Mirach had been so eager to usher me out, they didn't respond to what I said. Neither did Canopus, the one who prioritized my safety at every turn.

Nobody even attempted to respond at all.

◇ ◇ ◇

Canopus said nothing.

Mirach said nothing.

Their faces were twisted into a grimace I'd never seen before as they stared silently at Sirius.

Sirius gazed back at them, also saying nothing, before turning his head stiffly in my direction.

"Actually, Serafina, could you stay a little longer?"

"What? Really?!" I asked.

All the other knights responded before Sirius could. "Yes, please! Stay!"

"Yay! Thank you! I've got looooots of magic stored up from reading books all day. I'll try to be of help!"

How nice! The knights were accepting me. But when I smiled and tried to insist that I would be useful, they didn't smile back. In fact, their faces remained blank as they squinted at me in silence.

"She still has more?" one of them said finally.

"Unbelievable," said another.

They were the ones who told me to stay, so it was kind of weird how they were moaning about it now. Weren't they supposed to be happy? *Oh, well,* I told myself. I guess they were exhausted.

Meanwhile, Sirius sighed above me. "I thought I had a measure of your strength, but no... Compared to that time at the Forest of Lent, you're dealing with so many more targets across a greater distance." After that, he seemed to get his thoughts in order. "Canopus, Mirach!" he shouted. "You two guard Serafina at all costs! Don't hesitate to call for me if you think she's in danger!"

"Yes, sir!"

Then Sirius crouched down, looking me square in the eye. "Serafina, your support means everything," he said solemnly. "I promise that we will give you victory, our saint."

"Wow!"

As I was reeling from this weighty-sounding promise, the knights all shouted in unison: "We also pledge victory to you!"

"Whoa! Um, okay! I'll do what I can to assist!"

Basically, I have to support the knights as much as I can so they can beat up the monsters here, I thought as I watched Sirius dash into battle.

But all my resolve went to waste because I didn't have the chance to do a single thing after that. With just the Invigorate spell, the knights were able to overpower the ringed demon lions. All I really had to do was patch up some light scratches.

"Whoa! Why's it going in so deep?" Scheat shouted excitedly as his sword sank all the way into a demon lion's belly. "This is easier than cutting bread!"

"What a funny coincidence!" Miaplacidus chimed in. "I was just thinking this was like slicing butter!"

They traded impressions for a while—it looked like they were on the same page.

"Heh, this is awesome!"

"So *this* is how strong I can be with fifty percent more attack and speed!"

Mirach, who'd been listening in on the conversation some distance away, grumbled in reply, "You know this, Scheat, and yet you're always late to morning practice. And you always leave right when your shift is over, Miaplacidus."

I can't blame them, I thought. Scheat got sleepy in the mornings because he was young (according to him), and Miaplacidus was simulating newlywed life by going home straight after work (according to him).

Meanwhile, the other knights were also enjoying some light banter. This was nice to see—it meant that they were back to their usual selves. They had chatted through all the other battles outside of this one, after all.

"But y'know, it sure is weird fighting a demon lion that can only use one arm. It's crazy how much weaker they are."

"Hey, you were in the same boat before Princess Serafina healed you! I bet the demon lions were thinking *you* were nothing special."

Erm, judging by how they were insulting each other, they seemed to be in a good mood. And they showed it by finishing off almost half the monsters just a short while after I cast my magic.

Just like everyone had agreed at the start, Scheat landed the finishing blows. He always made sure to do his town's prayer sign and watch the shadow off—I could see his respect and reverence for the deceased. Some of the shadows were probably his friends from Zios Village, but he kept his emotions in check and stayed calm from start to finish.

Just once, though, his tough front crumbled. His whole body shook, and silent tears fell down his cheeks. He gave a longer prayer than usual, and when the shadow disappeared into the sky, he kept staring up there for a while.

It made me think that the shadow might have belonged to someone in his family.

None of the other knights said anything about it, but they put a lid on their cheery banter right then. I bet they were being considerate of Scheat.

Meanwhile, the demon lions were proving themselves to be pretty smart—maybe it was because they were monsters from the legendary Lodrigone Continent. As soon as they realized that I was the only healer, they all focused their attacks on me. But I did what Mirach said and stayed as close to him as I could. He and Canopus were both seasoned bodyguards, and they stopped the monsters' fangs and claws from coming anywhere close to me. Not to mention that Sirius and a bunch of the other knights came running straight away, forming a tight cluster around me.

"Wow, what tight security! It's like I'm an important princess!" I blurted out.

"You *are* our important princess!" Mirach pointed out matter-of-factly.

Oh, right.

Now that the monsters were concentrated in one spot, it made them easier to attack all at once.

To cut a long story short...the knights took out every single ringed demon lion before long. When the last beast fell, Sirius and the knights put a hand to their chests—the formal knight's salute—as they watched the final shadow ascend.

I put a hand to my chest too, and prayed that the trapped shadow would find the freedom to go wherever their heart took them.

◇ ◇ ◇

Once everything was over, Sirius walked over to me with a look of uncertainty on his face. This made me worried.

"What's the matter?" I looked up at him. "Did something bad happen?"

"Yeah, I screwed up a bit. I forgot how your magic can turn people into unbeatable warriors. And I never imagined that you would keep your promise so faithfully."

"Huh?" I cocked my head, not understanding what he was saying.

"You're always doing things I ask you not to, like falling asleep early or licking snack crumbs off your hands. I thought you were only staying quiet for those three minutes because you were too frightened to move."

"Whaaaat? That's not nice to say! I'm *always* serious!" I retorted.

But nobody agreed with me.

In fact, everyone, including Sirius, was deathly silent.

Uh-oh. Was this what I deserved for being naughty and breaking little promises like any girl my age? Everyone had been showering me with praise, but I'd gone and ruined it since the knights were all well aware of my reputation.

"W-w-well, I'm serious enough to keep a promise that's important to you," I insisted, to which Sirius responded by giving me a pat on the head.

"I'm sorry for underestimating you," he said, crouching down and peering at my face. "And...thank you. It's because of you that we didn't lose a single knight. We even managed to wipe out the ringed demon lions."

"Eh heh heh! You did it yourselves! My knights are all suuuuper strong!" I chirped. I couldn't help but start gushing about the knights even though Sirius knew how good they were already, seeing as he'd picked them for my royal guard and all.

Sirius was nice enough to give me a big nod. "Yes, very," he agreed with me. "I never imagined how powerful they could become."

"Tee hee hee hee!"

I was so delighted by the praise that I didn't even notice that the knights had all gathered around me until they all took a knee. *Huh?* I thought, looking at them in surprise. Did everyone hurt their knees?

Right then, Sirius took my hand. "Deneb, allow me to do a proper introduction. This is Serafina, the *saint* whom you and the Royal Red Shield are sworn to protect."

He showed off the back of one of my hands, which gleamed with a brilliant red pact sigil.

Seven, who normally kept himself hidden when I was around other people, cheerfully zoomed around in plain sight.

Captain Deneb looked straight at me, his expression grave and serious. "Is 'saint' a fitting word for you? Frankly, I was uncertain about what to call you after you wielded spells I'd never seen nor heard of before. But I can say this for certain: You made us as strong as demons."

As he spoke, he bowed his head low—an eye-opening sight.

"Wh-what happened, Captain Deneb?" I was gobsmacked. "Lift your head this instant!"

But the captain kept his head to the ground. "As the man entrusted with this royal guard, please allow me to thank you for ensuring every knight's survival. I am truly grateful from the bottom of my heart."

"Thank you so much, Princess Serafina!" all the knights declared in unison, right after Captain Deneb said his piece.

They were so loud that it kind of hurt my ears, but I managed to stop myself from wincing.

Captain Deneb then lifted his head slowly. He squinted at the back of my hand as if it was a blinding sight. "A red sigil, hm? I've never seen one so vivid before, nor one that appears only when the user summons their spirit. Everything about you defies my understanding, Princess Serafina. Please allow me to analyze your powers with a fine-tooth comb."

I had no idea, but apparently spirit pact sigils had ranks, and red was the highest among them. Oh, and the sigils were always visible on the back of the owner's hand. Since I was ignorant about it all, what Captain Deneb said sounded totally ridiculous to me.

My eyes went wide. "You...want to go over them with a fine-tooth comb?!" I asked shakily.

He nodded back at me with a very serious expression. "It has been over twenty days since I was assigned to this post, and in all that time, I failed to recognize your talents. For that, I am deeply ashamed. Please give me the chance to learn about you."

"But, um, I'm sure you'll just be disappointed..." I said in a small voice.

Captain Deneb just smiled at me, though. He didn't take back what he said. Looking at him, I had to say...I got the feeling that he'd never back down. I hadn't realized what a stubborn guy he was—he was a fearsome foe indeed.

I bet he'd soon find out about my meager skills and roll his eyes at me...

◇ ◇ ◇

That night, Scheat visited my room.

When I let him in, wondering what this was about, he didn't bother closing the door behind him. He stood in the middle of the room and bowed his head low.

"I was able to free my family and friends from the monsters because of you, Princess Serafina. I'll never be able to thank you enough."

Oh dear! I waved my hands, flustered. "No, I just did my part, that's all. Everyone else did great too. Plus, nobody worked harder today than you, Scheat."

Scheat knelt on one knee so that he was down to my eye level. "That's all you can say after everything you did? You really are an amazing one, Your Highness," he said earnestly. "I'm proud to be at your side."

"Oh, um! Thank you." I didn't argue back.

Scheat was being unusually modest today. Maybe he was humbled from seeing the shadows of his friends and family. I had to be as nice as possible to him.

He looked straight into my eyes. "You taught me that I'm not nearly as strong as I think. Your attack and speed buffs gave me a taste of where I'd be after three more years of training. It's what let me defeat the ringed demon lions."

When Scheat told me last night that he wanted to become strong, he was talking about getting there through his own efforts. It made me worry that he wouldn't appreciate my help, so his sunny expression came as a relief.

"You're not mad, Scheat! I'm glad I wasn't making a nuisance of myself."

"Perish the thought, Princess Serafina. I'm nothing but grateful," Scheat declared.

I could see he was saying what he truly felt. I was glad that he was such an earnest person. "You're so honest, Scheat," I said, feeling warm and fuzzy inside. "And you're super strong too! Stay by my side, okay? I feel safe when you're around."

Throughout these past few days, when Scheat had been possessed by the need to avenge his hometown, I'd been worried that he would leave my royal guard. So I took advantage of this moment to beg him to stay.

This made Scheat's cheeks turn pink, a rare sight for him. "You're saying that to *me*? Oh, Princess Serafina, I'm really, truly blessed to have you as my liege. I hope I can serve you until the end of time."

"Tee hee hee! Okay, be my knight forever! Oh, right!" I clapped my hands as I just remembered something.

"What is it?" Scheat asked curiously. "I'll do anything in my power for you as your knight."

This sounded promising, I thought, so I went ahead and told him my idea. "Okay, why don't you take some time off for yourself tomorrow? You could pay your respects at Zios Village."

The thought came to me because Scheat's hometown was so close by.

Upon hearing my suggestion, Scheat gave me a long, hard stare. "Your Highness, you certainly have a habit of saying the unexpected. You've done more than enough for me already, yet you're still so considerate? I didn't realize it at the time, but you made an incredibly effective potion for Canopus as well. And now you're extending your kindness to me. No member of royalty would go so far for an ordinary knight."

"What?" My eyes widened. "But you're not an ordinary knight—you're *my* knight." Of *course* I'd be worried about him.

"Exactly," Scheat said solemnly. "*I'm* the one who's meant to support *you*. It's supposed to be a unilateral relationship. I hope you can accept my devotion and respect."

I frowned, not really understanding his big words. Scheat smiled sheepishly.

"Thank you, Princess Serafina," he said after a pause. "I know you made your offer from the heart, and I appreciate it. Tomorrow, I'll go pay my respects."

With that, he lowered his head again.

His words sent a jolt through me. "Scheat, do you suppose that the shadows you freed went back to their graves?"

Scheat was silent for a moment, his head still pointed at the floor. "It was a terrible pity, but one of my family members was captured in the shadow of a demon lion," he said, not looking up. "It was my older brother. He was a responsible fellow with a good head on his shoulders. It was because of him that I got away when Zios Village was attacked twelve years ago."

Scheat cut himself off there and took a deep breath to calm down before he resumed.

"I think my brother was the first to die. He protected my father, mother, and sister, and that's why he was the only one of my family to get captured. He was...a great man. He had the misfortune of falling captive, but seeing him again was how I knew that he stopped the demon lions from taking the others. I'll look up to him till the day I die."

"Yeah, your big brother sounds like a really amazing person!" I nodded back eagerly.

Scheat lifted his head and peered at me.

There were tears in his eyes.

"His dream...was to become a knight. He was always saying how he wanted to leave the village and become a knight in the capital. So I swear I'll become a knight who won't bring any shame upon his elder brother. When I see him again in the afterlife, I'll hold my head high and tell him, 'I was a knight.'"

When Scheat said that, he was the coolest he'd ever been.

I bet he was already the kind of knight that his brother would be proud of.

"Scheat, you're already plenty cool! He's going to be so happy the next time you see each other!"

For some reason, Scheat's face turned red when he heard what I said. He blinked tremblingly, and a tear streaked down his cheek. He'd been holding it in this whole time.

"Huh? What's wrong?" I asked.

"That's what I want to know! The heck...? I've never gotten like this from hearing praise before, not from anyone... Princess Serafina, I'm going to have to ask you to stop giving me new emotions!"

"Uh, okay!" I answered, although I had no idea how I was supposed to achieve that.

Just when I was thinking that maybe I ought to change the subject, I remembered something Lyra said on the way back from the forest.

"Oh, right, I heard from Lyra that the 'shocking' in your nickname from when you were little didn't mean 'sign of danger,' it meant 'sign of an unbelievable hottie.'"

"What?"

Scheat's eyes widened, like he'd just had a giant revelation.

"It's 'cause you're good-looking and have an eye-catching appearance. Lyra said you were like that since you were little. The boys were sad that you weren't a girl, and that's how they came up with that nickname."

"Those brats!" Scheat grumbled, his eyebrows slanted down, and he looked like he was about to cry. "I'll give them a good talking-to at their graves tomorrow."

When Scheat said that, he seemed to be remembering his hometown fondly.

I was happy for him—he was finally coming home.

Right then and there, I made a decision: I would visit the Set Villa every year so that Scheat would never run out of opportunities to pay his respects.

As I watched Scheat go, the moon's gleaming light came shining in through the window. I felt like this beautiful world around me was supporting me in my decision, and a tingle of happiness ran through my body.

And so I prayed... Let my knights be happy and healthy. Always and forever.

Serafina's Ring

AS I WALKED ALONG the beach, I spotted some people out and about. It looked like we'd left the private beach for the royal family. The people were wearing bright and colorful clothing, which made for a fun atmosphere.

When I cast my gaze wider, I noticed half a dozen simple tents, their roofs fluttering in the wind. I wandered closer, curious what the fuss was about. It turned out that they were stalls with all kinds of goods for sale.

"Oh, how cute!"

One of the shops was a jeweler, and it had a bunch of glittering gems with different colors.

As my eyes were drawn to the display, the stall owner called out to me: "Hey, young lady! We've got some special jewels today. Why don't you come have a look?"

"Wow, they're all so pretty!"

Red, pink, purple, orange, green, light blue, dark blue—so many different gems were sparkling in the sunlight. I thought they were all really neat, although my hand was drawn to one item in particular: an adorable ring studded with more than ten jewels.

"Sirius!"

I flashed him a big smile, only for my eyes to meet his stony face. "Serafina, you can see from miles away that this is a shoddy product. Just say the word, and I can get you a much nicer ring."

"Really?"

That reminded me of how Sirius gave me a hair accessory the other day. It had a yellow jewel as big as a bird's egg in it, which made it heavy to wear. Then there was the sword-shaped brooch he gifted me. It had dozens of glittering, clear-colored jewels in it, but they twinkled so much in the light that wearing it hurt my eyes. The ladies-in-waiting stored these things *very* carefully, so I guess they were super expensive...but to be honest, I didn't feel like they were meant for little girls.

"Sirius, I want the ring with lots of sparkling little jewels!"

He went pale. "You want that ring with *those* tiny little excuses for jewels? Each one is about half the size of your pinkie nail."

"Yep! I love how cute and tiny they are!"

"It's severely lacking in design sense. The size and colors don't match at all, it's clearly been slapped together."

"But it's soooo cute!"

Sirius stared at me and said, "Are you serious?"

Well, yes. I was serious from the start.

I didn't know much about jewelry, but there was an obvious difference between this store and the one Sirius went to in the capital. But Sirius still insisted on comparing them as if they were on the same level.

"This place might be different from the one you know, Sirius, but they made the perfect thing for me."

"The perfect thing? This?"

Uh-oh. Was Sirius being rude to the stall owner? I cast a worried look at the man. But when he looked at Sirius and saw his fine, neatly trimmed fingernails, his top-quality clothing, and the magic stone-studded sword in his decorative scabbard, he silently turned to look in the direction we came from. A wave of understanding washed over his face when he saw that the path we took was connected to the royal family's private beach. It caused him to shake his head in defeat, as if Sirius's attitude was only to be expected.

On one hand, it was a good thing that the owner avoided causing a fuss because he figured out who Sirius was from his appearance, but on the other hand, it meant that Sirius had completely failed at the "concealing his identity" part of his plan. I couldn't help but give him an annoyed look, but he didn't seem to notice.

"Okay, I'll get it for you," he said, pulling a coin out of his trouser pocket.

But when he placed the coin on the store owner's hand, the man's eyes boggled. "A p-platinum coin?! Is this...real?! I-I can't give you change for this."

"But that's all I have on me." Sirius added, "I don't like carrying a bunch of coins around, so I only keep one in my pocket. It can pay for most things."

He muttered that last part to me as a sort of apologetic explanation.

Then he said thoughtfully to the store owner, "Okay, how much else do I need to buy so you don't have to give any change."

"The entire stock, I'm afraid."

Sirius said nothing.

If it had been only one or two things, Sirius would probably have let me pick and choose, but he didn't seem keen on buying over a hundred things. His eyes swept over all the rings, bracelets, and necklaces in deep thought.

Then his eyes met with the stall owner next door, who had been watching the whole scene in concern. She was selling bread in the shape of turtle legs. "This is my wife," the jewelry store owner explained.

After saying his hellos, Sirius said, "All right," and turned to the woman. "Instead of giving me change, could you put the money toward feeding the children playing on the beach?"

"What?"

Sirius must have remembered how we passed a bunch of children eagerly trying to catch fish on the way here. They did mention how hungry they were. While the parents ran the stalls, the kids were likely hard at work too. Sirius was probably worried about them staying hungry all the way till dinner.

"But the bread is cheap. We'd be feeding the children for a month," said the stall owner.

"Yes, I suppose the children would be upset when they stop getting their supply after being fed that long," Sirius said brusquely. "If they take a liking to it, then you're sure to get regular business."

Sirius hated it when people said he was nice, so he tried to avoid being thanked by speaking in a curt tone. Despite this, his kindness shone through anyway. The jewelry store man and his bakery owner wife showed it by fervently shaking Sirius's hand.

"I know some of the local knights around here. I'll get them to come over to keep an eye on things every so often and handle the money each month," Sirius went on, not meeting the couple's eyes.

Oblivious to Sirius's discomfort, the stall owners shouted in excitement. "Wow, you're acquainted with the knights?!"

"Just having the knights around the store will keep the ruffians in check! What a boon!"

They weren't "acquaintances" so much as subordinates, just like every knight in the country who wasn't Commander Wezen. I shot an exasperated look at the second-top knight in the nation—he was chewing on the turtle leg bread in a deliberately rough manner.

Erm, it was kind of pointless for him to stop minding his manners when the stall owners had already seen right through him. The couple was probably thinking the same thing I was as they watched him with strained politeness.

"Thanks, Sirius!" I said as we walked back to the villa ten minutes later. "I'll take care of it forever!"

But Sirius just scowled at my smile. "You like it that much? That thing?" He grumbled. "Seems like a worthless trinket to me."

I didn't care, though. I stretched out my hand and admired the ring on my finger. "Tee hee hee! It's pretty!"

"I suppose it doesn't matter whether it meets my standards as long as you see the value in it. But I'm not letting you marry a worthless man."

The knights, who had been watching from some distance away, approached us now that we had left the stalls. They cocked their heads at Sirius's words.

"What a funny thing to say. Nobody other than the king himself would live up to *your* standards, Vice-Commander Sirius."

"He's basically dooming the princess to a life of eternal singledom! Oof, the poor girl."

I looked back at Sirius. "Oh, so I might never get married? That's okay, I can spend my life with Sirius," I said happily.

Sirius smiled like he thought that was funny. "I'd be looking after you forever, then? I don't mind." He cast a deliberate glance at my ring finger. "I'm just glad it doesn't take much to please you, just a single ring—and not a very good one at that."

"Tee hee! I don't need anything else as long as I can be with you and Seven."

Sirius put on an exaggerated frowny face. "That's a very kind of offer, but I doubt you'll feel the same way when you're older. Don't worry, I'm fully prepared for the day you ditch me."

"Sirius!" I huffed at his cheeky face.

Right then, I heard the pattering sound of footsteps behind me.

What's this? I turned around and saw a handful of children chasing after us. When they reached us, they stopped and bowed.

"Thanks for the turtle bread, Mister!" they said with smiles.

"It's super yummy."

"We really appreciate it!"

When Sirius replied by simply raising his hand, the children ran off, their faces still grinning widely. Feeling all warm and fuzzy from inside seeing so many kids around my age smiling, I reached out and clasped Sirius's hand.

Slowly, we walked back to the villa, hand in hand.

My ring sparkled under the setting sun. When I saw how brilliantly it shone, it crossed my mind that Sirius had truly given me something beautiful.

Serafina Becomes Sirius's Daddy

"OH, SERAFINA, you're especially adorable today! How do you maintain your exquisite cuteness every single day?" Father gushed at the breakfast table.

This was just business as usual for him, so Mother, Shaula, and Sirius went on eating without paying him any attention.

But I stared up at Father and asked the question that was on my mind. "Why do you praise me every day?"

"Clever girl! That's a great question!" Father's face was already looking goofy because of his gushing, and it only got goofier. He seemed *that* pleased about being asked a question. "It's because you're unbelievably cute, of course! I'm an honest man, so I call it exactly as I see it."

"Honesty is all well and good, but there are many occasions when it's more prudent to refrain from speaking your mind, especially given that you are a king. I am sure that many would prefer you keep your thoughts to yourself." Sirius smoothly offered his advice (?) without even pausing in his meal.

But Father continued as if he hadn't heard. "And I'm your father, Serafina. It's my job to praise you and make people see what's great about you."

"Your job...?"

Ah, okay. I nodded in understanding. True, you didn't always have the opportunity to praise someone outside your family.

It made me wonder if anyone ever praised Sirius. I glanced at him. Even a kid like me could tell that he had a nice face. He was cool and kind, and he was the strongest knight in the entire kingdom!

Sadly, his mother and father had already passed away. Plus, his mother was from the distant Arteaga Empire, and her side of the family lived over there. Since his father only had one brother—my father—we were pretty much the only people he could call family.

Maybe my family should praise Sirius...

"Father, you said you were an honest man, right? When you see someone worthy of praise, you feel like you have to say something nice about them. Why don't you say nice things to Sirius, then?" I asked, tilting my head.

Father instantly scowled. "What's there to say? He's the next-best-looking after me? Or that he's only half as strong as I was when I was nineteen?"

Shaula gave Father a dry look. "Did you hear that, Mother? Some honest man he is."

"I always knew your father had a different idea of honesty compared to the average person."

I didn't really know what Shaula and Mother were getting at, but Father's words were easy to understand.

"I get it, Father. You wouldn't praise someone if you were more amazing than them."

There was silence after that…and then Mother snapped at Father for something, but I didn't really listen to what they were saying. The idea of a "job" was swirling in my head.

That evening, I visited Mother's room and asked her questions about Sirius's father.

"What kind of person was he?"

"Lord Achernar, the previous Duke Ulysses? Let's see, he was a very compassionate and wise person." Mother peered out the window, her eyes softening in recollection. "He had a frail constitution and spent most of his days in bed, but he never let that get to him. He was always optimistic, always looking for something he could do."

In my mind's eye, I saw a large, gentle-looking man stroking a mini Sirius on the head.

"Did he get along with Sirius?" I asked the question I was most curious about.

Mother nodded and smiled. "Everyone could see how deeply Lord Achernar cared for Sirius. He was always saying how proud he was of his son, and he showed it too in his actions."

I could see that he did the job of a father, just as my own father explained it. But since he had passed away, and since my father was too good to be the replacement, nobody was around to praise Sirius.

That meant the job fell to me!

With my newfound calling in mind, my ideas started to take shape.

That same night, I waited for Sirius in his room, but his quarters were so nice and warm that I found myself nodding off...

"Are you awake, Serafina?" a voice called out to me.

When I opened my eyes, Sirius was peering at me in the bed.

"You were already dozing off by the time I got back here. I thought you'd wake up after a little while, but then you actually fell asleep. I was just wondering whether I should carry you to your room or let you sleep here."

I only had one thing to say to that: "I'm not Serafina," I muttered.

A deeply wary look came over Sirius's face. "What? Don't tell me we're doing that quiz again."

He was referring to the "copycat quiz" we did in his office the other day. I pretended to be a butterfly, but he didn't catch on to it at all and got very upset. This was probably why he sounded so reluctant to do it all over again.

"No," I insisted as I rubbed my eyes. "I'm your daddy now. That's why I was sleeping in your bed."

"You're my father? Why would you hog your son's bed?" Sirius asked in confusion.

At that point, my eyes were finally wide open. "Your daddy was sickly and in bed all the time, right? I was trying to be like him," I explained.

Sirius frowned. "I see. I never would have dreamed you were copying my father from the ferocious way you kicked that blanket."

I grinned back at him. "Heh heh heh. But remember how I cheered you up with words that sounded like they came from your daddy? You said a close relative like me must be just like him. So, when you think about it, I was like your daddy!"

"That is a frightening leap of logic. But I couldn't very well tell you otherwise. I suppose this is what I deserve for letting you think that way."

Sirius sounded like he was agreeing with me, so I seized my chance to get in some praise.

"Okay, so, I...you know, your daddy...think that you are great! You're especially great today! And you're great every day! Daddy is soooo proud of how great you are!"

Sirius listened to my gushing in silence. Then, with a completely straight face, he muttered, "I can totally see how you're the king's daughter."

"Huh? What did you say?" I asked, since I didn't really hear him.

"Oh, nothing, Serafina..." Sirius began, but I was his daddy right now, not Serafina. So I just stared at him, not responding to that name.

Eventually, after a long silence, Sirius corrected himself. "No, Father." He sounded deeply resigned. "I was just wondering why you decided to praise me so suddenly."

"Ahem. Because it's a father's job, of course! A father is meant to praise you and get people to understand what's good about you."

"I see. And since nobody has been fulfilling that role recently, you decided to step up to the task."

"Yup. You might think it doesn't need to be said, but it's still a daddy's job! And you really are a wonderful person!"

I smiled, but this only made Sirius's lip curl down. He put me on his knee and rested his head into my neck. "Serafina...no, Father, yes? Don't spoil me too much. It'll make me weak when I'm supposed to be strong enough to protect you."

"Then it's a weakness you need. Don't you worry. I'll be there to protect you when you're weak..."

Just as I was saying what needed to be said, the drowsiness hit me again. Sirius grabbed me by the sleeve, but I still lost to the sleepiness and collapsed on the bed.

"Are you sleepy, Serafina?" I heard Sirius's voice. "Why don't you stay here for tonight?"

Judging by his tone, he wanted us to snooze together. He was telling me that I could stay right where I was and he wouldn't chase me out.

"That sounds nice. This is Daddy's bed, after all. And Daddy wants to sleep with his son tonight."

"I know you're doing your best to play my father's part, but you're already off the mark. I've slept alone for as long as I can remember."

"Eh heh heh. Then this'll be a first. Your first time falling asleep with Daddy Serafina."

He paused and said, "I see, so this will be a day to remember."

I was fast asleep before he even finished his sentence. So I didn't hear what he said after that.

"I'm supposed to be a full-fledged knight. How pathetic of me to lean on a six-year-old. I could never tell a soul... Well, I'm sure that Serafina will kick the blanket a lot in her sleep, so I'd better sleep close by to make sure it stays on."

I was comfy and had a good night's sleep because there was a warm body next to me the whole time.

"So warm... You're a good boy, Sirius," I mumbled sleepily, still wanting to play the role of his father.

Maybe I was dreaming, because he didn't say a word of complaint. In fact, he stroked my head as if he couldn't be happier with me...which convinced me that this had to be a dream. I fell back asleep, not questioning a thing.

I was comforted, knowing that the Sirius who always put on a tough face had a softer side to him too.

A Tale of the

Secret Saint

ZERO

POINT OF VIEW

SIRIUS

Serafina's Former Greedy Room...

"ARE YOU THERE, Serafina?"

When I visited Serafina's room after dinner, as per my usual habit, I was greeted with an unusual silence.

Thinking that she was absent, I was about to leave when I noticed papers had been placed around her room. Silently, I walked over to a sheet and picked it up.

"Here, this is a book."

The paper was stuck on the bookshelf, explaining something that didn't need to be explained.

Okay, I thought. Although I had no desire to read a book, I figured she was telling me to pick one from the bookshelf. Serafina played many inscrutable games, and this was just one of them.

So I picked a book she would like from the shelf. Then a sudden thought occurred to me, and I decided to say the title aloud. "*The Red-Headed Princess and the Golden Knight.* Yes, I'll go with that one."

Predictably, a stream of girlish giggles erupted from the corner of the room. Serafina was hiding nearby, just as I anticipated.

Well, if that was the case, then my hand was forced. I'd play along until she was satisfied.

So I collected the next paper. Out of consideration for the listener in the room, I read it aloud: *"Here, this is a blanket."* It was placed on the bed. "A cozy blanket, hm? It certainly seems big enough to make Serafina nice and snug."

"Tee hee hee."

The paper on the table said, *"Here, this is a snack."*

"I'm not a big fan of sweet things, so I'll pass."

"Grrrrrrrrr!"

I hastily corrected myself. "But, well, I suppose I'm in the mood today. I'll take one for the road."

"Tee hee hee."

And so, by the time I reached Serafina, my hands were full carrying a book, a blanket, and a plate of cookies.

Although she was ostensibly in hiding, she crept her way over to the sofa at some point, completely exposing her cover. But because I could imagine her wailing "How did you know?!" if I pointed this out, I pretended not to notice her. Honestly, if I had truly been unable to notice her blatant movements, I would have been a failure of a knight.

And so, after taking note that Serafina was sitting on the sofa, I made my way over to where she was and made a very deliberate exclamation: "What? You're here, Serafina?"

Alas, my tone sounded all too insincere even to my own ears. Not a good sign. *I really have no talent in this department,* I thought as I gazed down at Serafina.

My eyes were drawn to the piece of paper she'd pasted over her entire face.

"Here, this is Serafina."

"Well, this is a tricky one to explain," I muttered. "Ah, wait, I've got it. I don't need to explain what's on the paper, it's just letting me know what Serafina wants me to pick up."

I put the other things I was holding on the table and carefully removed the paper stuck to Serafina, revealing her face to the world. Her eyes were scrunched shut.

"Good evening, Princess." I sat on the sofa and put Serafina on my knee.

I waited for a short while, but the cheeky young girl refused to open her eyes.

My hand was forced, then. "Hm, I've got a hankering for picture books right now," I muttered to myself. "Guess I'll start reading one."

I kept Serafina on my knee and started reading her favorite book aloud, but she stubbornly kept her eyes closed. So I stopped reading and chuckled...a chuckle which also sounded incredibly forced.

"Ha ha. Did you know that a picture book is three times better if you look at the pictures?"

Serafina finally opened her eyes, and I swiftly took the opportunity to present a cookie in front of her mouth.

"Eat up, Princess. Don't you love sweet things?"

Serafina obligingly opened her mouth wide to accept the cookie and immediately started chewing once I tossed it inside.

"Mmmm! Yummy!"

She finally made her first peep.

I breathed a sigh of relief and said, "You turned your room into a series of tasks for me. If I had to give it a name, it would be... Serafina's Greedy Room?"

"Mm quite," she said, her mouth still full of cookie. "Ish Sirimyus's Gweedy 'oom."

"It's what?"

Serafina hastily swallowed her snack and tried again. "Not quite. It's Sirius's Greedy Room."

"You think I want to drape a blanket over myself, read a picture book, and shovel cookies into my mouth?!"

"Nuh-uh. You wanna wrap me in a blanket and feed me cookies as you read me a picture book, right?"

I was speechless for a moment.

"Well, yes." I nodded frankly—after all, she was right on the money. "I see, so...this room is one where I can act on my desires and spoil you?"

"That's right!"

When I saw Serafina's bright smile, I knew in my heart that I would never be able to win against her.

All things considered, it may have seemed like a humble desire, but...when I thought about it, perhaps it was too much to ask for. I was always going to smile whenever I thought about Serafina's idea of a "Sirius's Greedy Room."

This girl never failed to surprise me.

A Tale of the Secret Saint ZERO

POINT OF VIEW

SIRIUS

The Tragic Tale of the Poetry Recital, Act Two

FRANKLY, I HAD A BAD FEELING. I could only curse my foolishness for not making up some excuse to leave the room the moment I entered.

But there's no point crying over spilled milk, as they say.

The king, who sat next to me, turned his smiling face in my direction. "Isn't this exciting, Sirius? I can't wait to see what Serafina has in store for us! I'm certain my adorable little girl will have an impressive show."

Indeed. I was being made to sit in on Serafina's school presentation.

It was poor luck on my part that I happened to run into His Majesty in the corridor.

"Great timing, Sirius! Do you have a minute?"

Despite his extremely lackadaisical tone, he was the venerable monarch of this nation. I followed him and ended up in a grand hall with just two chairs placed in the middle. The queen was in one of the seats.

My eyes swept around the hall in surprise. There was a large curtain covering the wall along with a sign declaring "Princess Serafina's School Presentation." Ah yes, the tutors had mentioned that the king was asking about Serafina's progress. I assumed that they would hand him a written report, but it seemed that His Majesty was keen on turning it into an event.

At that point, I should have thought up some business to attend to and excused myself...but when my eyes fell on Serafina peeking out from behind the stage, she waved at me with a smile. I had no choice *but* to wave back.

And that meant staying put in the hall.

Stay calm, Sirius.

This was an audience for the king. Serafina's tutors must have picked suitable material and rehearsed this presentation with her numerous times. Surely this wasn't going to be a slapdash affair.

Somebody hurriedly brought over a third chair, and I sat down while taking some deep breaths. *This will be fine,* I told myself over and over.

Apparently, I was the only one who was nervous. The queen, who was seated to the king's other side, squealed in delight as she read through the program. "Oh, she's starting with a poetry recital!"

Flashbacks of a certain horrific poem ran through my mind, but I reminded myself that things would be different this time. *Surely the tutor had strenuously revised the poem to make it palatable for the royal couple,* I told myself optimistically.

Meanwhile, the king joined in on the gushing. "Oh, so it's titled *Parental Love, Like the Glittering Night Sky*. How touching! Just the title brings a tear to my eye..."

I breathed a sigh of relief at the king's words. The poetry tutor was evidently doing his job well. Given that he had shown enough foresight to prepare something suitable for the occasion, I doubted that I needed to worry about the actual poem.

My nervousness partially alleviated, I made myself comfortable in my chair.

At long last, the curtain lifted, revealing Serafina in an adorable dress. She greeted us with a little bow, but her jaw dropped when she saw me from the podium. She'd spotted me before, but she must have thought that I wouldn't stick around.

This told me that the presentation was meant solely for the royal couple. I was only here because I had the misfortune of bumping into the king, so perhaps it was for the best if I made myself scarce.

As I sat there fretting over my mistake, Serafina stroked her chin in thought for a short while before breaking out into a sunny smile.

"I'm changing the poem! Now it's *I Wanna Be Sirius*."

Startled cries rang out at Serafina's sudden declaration.

"What? S-Serafina, weren't you going to wax poetic about your daddy?!" the king cried.

"Y-Your Highneeeeeess!" The poetry tutor exclaimed, sounding like he was going to faint any second.

But Serafina broke out into a dance, completely undeterred. Her short limbs flailed in time with her words.

"I wanna be Sirius!
I wanna be Sirius!
Nom nom nom. I love to eat meat!
But oh no, I'm full! My stomach is beat!
I wanted more, it's so yummy!
I wish I had Sirius's big tummy!
I wanna be Sirius!
I wanna be Sirius!
Wow wow wow, my teacher's got a bald spot!
But I'm too short, I don't see a lot!
I would've given him a hat if it was in my sight!
I wish I had Sirius's height!"

When Serafina concluded her song, she gazed at me with sparkling eyes. I'd seen this often enough to know that she was waiting for praise. But sadly, Canopus wasn't here. Well, he probably *was* around, but in the wings so that he could easily protect Serafina on the stage.

I would have to tackle this dilemma all by myself.

"Serafina...um..."

I suspect that the wheels in my mind had never turned so furiously. Yet however much I racked my brain, I could not think of anything praiseworthy about Serafina's poem.

I decided to call upon our venerable monarch for aid. "Your Majesty! I leave it to you to highlight Serafina's great work!"

"What?!" The king was gobsmacked.

"Yay! Thank you, Sirius!" Serafina's delighted voice rang out simultaneously.

"S-Sirius!" The king called out my name with a wretched expression, but I refused to meet his eyes.

"Your Majesty, the princess has unveiled her talents." I reached a hand out. "Do you have any comments about her poem?"

"Urk... S-Serafina, you have...wonderful powers of observation! Great job on noticing how big and tall Sirius is! And, erm, the Arteagian language tutor's bald spot..."

Judging by the king's anguished expression, he was clearly grasping at straws.

"Your Majesty!" cautioned the head attendant standing behind him. "Princess Serafina did not specify the tutor."

"Oh, my apologies! Um, well, you certainly noticed that one of the tutors, whoever he is, has a bald spot. And it was very thoughtful of you to consider giving him a hat. What a nice girl you are! But I'm hoping that next time you will sing about your love for your daddy."

The king elegantly concluded with a request for the next poem. Now that was impressive. For the first time, I felt respect for my monarch.

I peered at Serafina, curious about her reaction. She was smiling, evidently pleased by the praise. What a relief. This was her moment in the spotlight, and I wanted her to revel in it.

I don't know whether my feelings got through to her, but she looked like she was having a lot of fun as she continued to present what she had learned to us.

Alas, my heart was terribly fickle. I couldn't bring myself to truly believe that she was a competent and able student. Instead, I kept waiting in suspense for the other shoe to drop.

When a subordinate came to fetch me about an emergency not long after the presentation resumed, I was honestly relieved. *"I had no choice. I'm not deserting under enemy fire, definitely not,"* I told myself as I pulled a sheepish face and left the room.

Serafina noticed my departure because she stopped her musical performance and waved me off with a smile. Needless to say, I felt terrible.

That night, when I went to Serafina's room for one of my usual visits, her table was laden with musical instruments and books.

A bad feeling came over me, and I asked her what this was about.

"You had to leave in the middle of my show, remember?" She smiled. "So I'll show you what you missed out on."

I struggled to respond. "I see," I said finally, "you have the compassion of an angel. But it's hard for me to accept such special treatment when I left out of my own selfish convenience. I'd like to witness the fruits of your studies at the next presentation, if I can make it there."

Even as I turned her down, the cold thought occurred to me that I was merely putting off the problem instead of addressing it. But the fact of the matter was that even watching a mere fraction of that presentation had worn me out. It wasn't hard to imagine that she would be that much more tired than me after showing off all that she had learned.

I held out a small pile of picture books to her as a peace offering. "Serafina, you did well today. And what I did see of your presentation was excellent. As thanks for letting me watch, I'll read these books for you tonight."

"Oh! Really?" Serafina happily took the books and started shuffling through them, looking for one for me to read.

"Yeah. I'm happy to read them all, but why don't you take a rest first? I'm sure you're tired."

"Nuh-uh! I've got plenty of energy! Okay, read them all for me, Sirius!"

As I watched Serafina snuggle under her blanket, I smiled and took a seat on the bed. Contrary to my expectations, however, she remained awake as I read aloud every book in the pile. She only dozed off after I finished the very last page.

I tucked her arm under the blanket and stroked her head. "Good night, Serafina. You were a hard little worker today."

That was good enough for today, I thought...although I regretted how I'd merely put off Serafina's school presentation for later.

I had no way of knowing that my future self would resent me for subjecting him to twice the stress when the second presentation came around.

A Tale of the Secret Saint ZERO

What If You Had an Invisibility Cloak?

My math tutor was a really smart person. He was Father's age and wore glasses, but sometimes he asked weird questions. He said, "Stimulating the imagination is part of studying," but...

"Princess Serafina, if you had a cloak that made it impossible for other people to see you, what would you do with it?"

"Um, I'd make Father think he's gaining weight."

"Er, care to explain?"

"I'd secretly jump on the scales when he's weighing himself so it says he's heavier than he actually is!"

The tutor made a face as if I'd dropped a one-of-a-kind math book into a river. "That's what you'd do with a rare, invaluable invisibility cloak? Play a petty prank?"

"Yep! I bet it'd be fun since he'd fall for it one hundred percent!"

My tutor said nothing for an awfully long while. Then he started muttering something over and over, like he was saying it more for himself than anyone else: "Diversity is important. I must respect different perspectives in my pursuit of knowledge."

This happened a lot. Whenever he got like this, it took some time for him to get out of his own little world. Since I figured I should leave him alone, I turned my eyes to my textbook and started working on the next question.

"So, yeah, that's what happened."

That night, when I told Sirius about my day, he gave me a look that was hard to figure out. "Is that so? I'm glad you're always having fun. Although I can't say I understand the purpose of a class that enables your mischievous spirit."

"Huh? What did you say?" I asked, since I got the feeling that what he said wasn't a nice thing.

Sirius shrugged. "I mean...You're walking a very fine line. The people around you are always enabling you and letting you do as you like, and I get the feeling that nobody is going to set you straight."

"Whaaat?" I exclaimed in surprise. "But I study so hard every day! I should be getting brainier by the second!"

"It's complicated. I'd be proud of you if that were the case, but a part of me also hopes you'll never change. You're perfect the way you are." Sirius praised me with an amused grin and then peered at my face. "Now is there anything else you'd like to do if you got your hands on an invisibility cloak?"

It was the same question the math tutor had asked. I gave it some thought. "Hmm... I'd share it with you when you want to cry."

Sirius frowned as if he didn't understand. "What do you mean?"

"Since you're a grown-up, you don't cry in front of other people. But it's sad to cry alone, you know? So when you want to cry, I'd hide us both away."

"I see," Sirius muttered quietly after a pause.

I took this as a sign of agreement. "Yep!" I went on eagerly. "I'm warm, so I bet your tears will dry up when I snuggle with you."

"Or I might feel so warm that I won't cry at all," Sirius said, before propping me on his knee and squeezing his arms around me.

"Sirius?" I asked, knowing that he hugged me tightly whenever he got emotional.

He buried his head on my shoulder. "You're the one spoiling me rotten... I've never relied on anyone but myself till now."

Sirius's downbeat voice sounded so funny to me, I couldn't help but laugh. "Tee hee hee! That's not what it means to get spoiled rotten. You're just getting to feel lots of different emotions now."

A jolt seemed to run through Sirius, and then slowly he started to relax. "Right. I suppose you *are* a brainy one." He lifted his head, showing a look of hesitation. "Yes, you're perfect the way you are. If I ever find an invisibility cloak, I'll be sure to give it to you."

"Oooh, that's a promise! Let's mess with Daddy's scale together!"

I clapped my hands in delight, which instantly put a scowl on Sirius's face. "Am I being part of the problem by enabling your pranks?"

"Huh? What did you say?"

"Er...I mean, I'm at fault for knowing what you'd do and not stopping you. Basically, I'm letting you stay the way you are," Sirius replied as he patted my head for a while.

The next day, Sirius found me and said, "It's not easy to get your hands on an invisibility cloak, so this'll have to do for now," and gifted me a fluffy white cloak.

It was so warm! I couldn't wait for winter to arrive.

BONUS STORY

The Royal Guard Boys' Club

"YOU'RE LATE, Scheat!"

When Scheat was the last one to show up at the restaurant, the fellow members of the Royal Red Shield were waiting for him.

Since forming the new royal guard, the knights would regularly meet up at a private room in a restaurant. They called these meetings "The Royal Guard Boys' Club." Since they shared information that was normally kept strictly confidential, Scheat made sure to close the door securely behind him before he took a seat.

"Sorry, I was having trouble with that 'Vice-Commander Tag' report. He made me submit a second one."

Scheat's explanation was greeted with a round of boos.

"You're still not in the clear, Scheat? I passed on the first try!" Miaplacidus was already in high spirits. "You just gotta aim for Vice-Commander Sirius's feelings!" he said confidently as he slung an arm around Scheat's shoulder.

"His feelings? You mean I gotta drone on about a knight's ideals or whatever?" Scheat cocked his head quizzically.

Mirach shook his head in ridicule. "Short-sighted as usual. The vice-commander's ideals are loftier than a mountain. Any ideas *you* spout will never reach his level, and your report will never pass if you go that route."

"Huh? Really? Then how'd you guys get off the hook?!" Scheat's eyes widened.

To which everyone in the room shouted in unison: *"He's the Ultimate Mother Hen!"*

This moniker for the vice-commander of the knight brigades was a sacred taboo within the force. Nobody would dare utter it unless they were drunk.

"Huh? O-oh! I get it!" A look of understanding dawned on Scheat's face.

"You need only extol praise on Princess Serafina under the guise of an apology essay," Canopus explained neatly. "Vice-Commander Sirius passed anyone who did that."

"Aaaaaargh! So *that* was the trick!" A frustrated Scheat slumped his head on the table.

The knights passed a round of drinks in his direction. "Ha ha ha ha ha! It sure was! Anyway, drink up! Now that you know the secret, passing tomorrow should be a cinch!"

"The weak have gotta resort to their own tricks! We can face the Ultimate Mother Hen as long as we band together!"

Pathetic as those lines sounded in isolation, everyone in attendance roared them in unison, making it all too clear that they were brothers-in-arms—the royal guard members got along together very well.

After that, the conversation cycled through miscellaneous topics—Vice-Commander Sirius, bodybuilding, the monsters they slayed the other day—before smoothly transitioning into the main subject at hand.

"But you know, our princess is such a sweetie! You hear that she commissioned a list of our names and portraits so she can remember all our names?"

"I heard, yeah. I actually snuck a look at the list, and my portrait was the handsomest by far!"

"Are you for real?! Your picture looked like a mutt to me!"

Laughter erupted across the table.

Nevertheless, anyone could read between the lines of the conversation and feel the knights' fondness for Serafina.

Despite the jovial mood, however, one knight voiced a note of disquiet. "But...Her Highness wasn't raised in the castle. I suppose there was some political reason for her to live in a separate villa since birth. Not that I mean to pry in the slightest, but I can't imagine that there were happy circumstances behind it."

Everyone glanced at Canopus when they heard this, but he just stared at the table, his lips drawn into a tight line. It was a huge giveaway that he knew the details—and that there *were* unhappy circumstances involved.

Just as a heavy silence fell over the gathering, Mirach broke in with a cheery tone. "All the more reason to protect Her Highness!"

He was exactly right.

"Yeah. No other royal would put in so much effort to remember our names. We're lucky to have her as our liege."

"*We* got picked for her guard. We gotta live up to those expectations!"

The knights all swore their fealty to Serafina, and with that, the boys' club meeting drew to a close.

Late that night, the group returned to the castle in the jolliest of moods—only for a familiar voice to cut through the darkness.

"Oh dear! Why are you up so late? Canopus, Scheat, Mirach, Miaplacidus..." The voice rattled off all their names.

"Princess Serafina?!" the knights exclaimed in surprise.

It was their liege, the one and only Serafina.

"What? Even the plants would be snoozing right now. Why are you still awake?!" Scheat shouted in astonishment.

Serafina grinned. "Tonight's a special night. Sirius is showing me glowing bugs as my reward for making a good song," she declared—and indeed, Vice-Commander Sirius was standing right behind her.

The knights all stared with wide, shocked eyes.

What on earth was going on? Their vice-commander didn't care a whit about pretty things, and yet here he was at Princess Serafina's beck and call, going out of his way to look at glow-in-the-dark bugs.

"Oof, now *that's* the Ultima—" Scheat began, no doubt under the alcohol's influence.

A fellow knight punched him swiftly. "Shut up, Scheat!"

"You got a death wish?!" another cried sharply.

Scheat blinked, realizing that he had just been on the verge of blurting out the boys' club talk. He shut his mouth and took a panicked step back. "S-sorry! The alcohol was making me say weird things."

Then, before anyone else could say "weird things" under the influence, the knights made a hasty retreat.

"Sorry for intruding on your fun!"

"Please excuse us!"

Everyone made their parting excuses one after another as they turned on their heels and ran.

"You guys were right!" Scheat cried once they were out of earshot. "The vice-commander has gotta adore the princess if he's willing to go out at night and look at glowing bugs with her. Ha ha ha, I see how to win him over! I'll add some praise about Her Highness to my report tomorrow! Then I'll be free!"

And Scheat actually did pass—on his fourth attempt after progressively scattering more compliments to Serafina across his report.

The Royal Guard Boys' Club was indeed a treasured reprieve for the ailing knights.

A Tale of the Secret Saint ZERO

Afterword

THANK YOU SO MUCH for picking up this book! We've now reached the second volume thanks to you all. Yay, this wasn't doomed to be a stand-alone!

The previous volume was mainly about filling in the gaps in the main story about the events from three hundred years ago, but this volume introduces new characters and a new story set within this world. Even in terms of physical locations, this volume covers a lot of new ground: beaches, towns, a spirit palace, and a new forest. Not bad for a heroine who only knew her one forest and a castle!

Out of all the new locations, we got a seaside scene for the front cover. Isn't it a lovely illustration? The characters look so vibrant, and the background is gorgeous! The color insert depicting the spirit palace has a wonderfully ethereal beauty as well. I couldn't help but give a slack-jawed stare when I first received the illustrations. Thank you so much, chibi-san, for always delivering such fantastic work!

Moving on, this was my first time trying to publish two books at the same time. This volume came out on the same date in Japan as Volume 8 of *A Tale of the Secret Saint*. I'm excited to see what the bookstores will be like with two books' worth of chibi-san's wonderful illustrations. I hope this can be a good opportunity for you to get into the main series if you haven't yet!

To celebrate the simultaneous release, we're holding a second character popularity poll. As the word "second" implies, there was a first one about six months ago. The winner was Captain Cyril of the First Brigade, a character exclusive to the main series, with 726 votes, and Sirius came in second with 581 votes. Similar to last time, we're planning to release a free short story about the top character on the Japanese publisher's website. Give your favorite character a vote if that piques your interest.* By the way, characters exclusive to *ZERO* like Scheat, Mirach, Miaplacidus, and Oligor are on the ballot as well.

I should also mention that I've started a Twitter account for announcements related to this series. There'll be a steady trickle of news, so check it out if you're interested.

https://twitter.com/touya_stars

Finally, I'd like to thank you all for reading this far. This series only took shape because of all the readers and other people who put in their tireless effort. I couldn't be more grateful.

My schedule was rather tricky this time with the simultaneous release, but I still had a lot of fun working on these books. I very much hope that you enjoy them.

* *Voting closed in February 2023.*